Goblins, Dames, Booze & Bullets

Memoirs from a Parallel Universe

Lawrence BoarerPitchford

Published by Lawrence BoarerPitchford, 2024.

GOBLINS, DAMES, BOOZE & BULLETS

First edition. April 1, 2024.

Copyright © 2024 Lawrence BoarerPitchford.

ISBN: 979-8988041719

Written by Lawrence BoarerPitchford.

Table of Contents

To K.N. Lee: Thank you for your support and faith in my work. You and your works of ficiton are a proof that success in the publishing business comes about with hard work, careful planning, and a mighty heart for those around you.

Also, to my friends like Gary, and family such as my wife, sisters, brothers, daughter, who have always been there to support my works. Much love to you all.

~Lawrence BoarerPitchford

Chapter 1

Crimson Snow

MAX LOOKED OVER AT the clock—nine hundred hours. His stomach growled loudly; it was about time to seek out some breakfast.

The light outside was dimming as the storm clouds charged the shore. For the moment the weather was taking a break, giving the surface of every street and building a respite from being coated with snow.

He looked at the vocalrelay; its silence had been nearly deafening over the past few days. He looked at the cost sheet for his local advertising budget. It was hard to believe that his efforts hadn't drummed up any clients. His mind drifted, and at certain points, it penetrated deep into that locked-away darkness he dreaded...his own past.

He stood, opened his desk drawer, removed his pistol, and set it on the tabletop. Then he went over and retrieved his long, dark wool overcoat. It would be a cold, windy walk from his office to the diner a few blocks over. He slipped the weapon into his coat pocket next to his gloves, put on his hat, exited his office, and locked the door behind him.

He opened the building's outer door to the street and felt the bite of the freezing air against his face. The unsettling quiet outside foretold of the coming snow, and as he stepped along the walkway, his snow boots crunched the icy covering with each stride.

A movement across the street caught his eye, and he narrowed his gaze. It was Tararill, one of the lovely working girls whom Max had gotten to know over the years. He had a soft spot for her. She always seemed optimistic and cheery for a female goblin living in Goblin Town.

Though she plied her trade to businessmen and philandering husbands, Max tried very hard not to make judgments. He was a human living in Goblin Town, and his history was checkered. Why would he cast aspersions on anyone else? He knew well that no one other than the soul in question could account for their path of successes and mistakes. He thought of her as a lost soul and rooted for her to find her path to a better way somewhere outside of this troubled part of the city.

She dashed along the sidewalk, her long legs churning up the snow behind her. Turning as if to run straight at Max, she momentarily looked behind her.

A loud pop echoed in the frozen air. Max instinctively dove to the side behind a parked steam cart. Ever since the war, the sound of a peroxide cartridge discharge made him seek safety without having to think long on the matter. Unfortunately, other things were known to make a similar sound.

He got to his feet and carefully looked over the cart. A tall fellow in a gray overcoat and hat was already halfway back to the far alley, almost skipping down the street. Tararill lay between two parked carts.

He rushed over and kneeled. The snow was so dark that it was almost black. A hole had been torn through her dark green coat. He ripped it open. She'd taken a lethal shot. Her two hearts pumped a flood of blood out of the wound and over her pinfeathers.

He pressed both hands on top of the hole and pushed down. The blood was pumping out between Max's fingers. He shouted to a passing prairie driver to fetch an ambulance and the police. The driver nodded and used his wireless to call for help.

Tararill looked up at the cloudy sky and shivered. "It's cold, Max..." Her voice was soft.

"Help is on the way. Keep talking to me. You're going to be okay."

Her voice was hoarse. "All I did was see what they were all bragging about."

"What was it?" Max pressed hard, but the blood kept coming.

"He showed them to me. Now, they killed me."

"Who did this?" Max's voice was filled with explosive passion.

Tararill held up her hand. In it was a crumpled piece of paper. "Here... Take it. I took it from his desk." She gasped and coughed. Some blood came from her mouth. "It is Har'ne the brood mother. She is right behind you in the light."

Max glanced over his shoulder. There was no one there. "Brood mother?"

"Brood mother... She's come to help me to the other side."
She looked at Max. "Thank you, Max, for always being nice to
me." She drew in a deep breath, exhaled, and was dead.

The loud clanging of the ambulance bells echoed from
down the street. Not far behind was the familiar sound of the
20th Precinct's siren. The constables were on the way too. Max
stood up. He took the paper from her limp hand and glanced
at it: "Balls. 1900 hours. Bring your bid."

Max walked over to the awning of the Chiky Bakery, went
under it and stamped his feet on the pavement to dislodge the
snow from his boots. Looking back at Tararill, he sighed then
took out his pipe with his bloody hand.

From his other pocket, he removed a bag of chawabak,
dipped the bowl into it, and then put away the sack along with
the note.

He bit down on the pipe stem, removed some matches,
and lit one. Drawing in the smoke, he watched the ambulance
coming down the slippery street. He blew out a plume of dark
gray into the air, then puffed a few times on the pipe making
the bowl glow red.

"Balls?" Max said softly into the scathing cold. He took
a few puffs then exhaled more gray smoke into the frigid air.
"What the shim does that mean?"

The ambulance arrived, steam pumping from the pressure
valves and smoke churning from the side stack. One of the
medics rushed to the rear and pulled out a stretcher.

He locked eyes with Max as he approached, then stopped
where Tararill lay. "Over here, Dale," the medic called.

Another medic came running with a leather bag of medical
tools. "Doesn't look good."

"You're too late. She's dead," Max said. "Shot through one of her hearts."

The ambulance driver stared down at Tararill as he shook his head. "Damn! She's pretty too. Such a waste. She can't be more than twenty."

"Twenty-two, to be exact," Max stated.

The constable cart arrived blasting all present with its loud whine. It crushed the frozen snow as it rolled to a halt, the flashing light on top alternating between blue and red. Several street constables got out.

A dwarf approached, his small hand resting on the rubber truncheon at his side. He wore a red jacket, blue pants, and white leather snow boots. Pinned to his pocket was his bronze wedge with a number stamped on it—the symbol of the law. He looked down at Tararill, kneeled, and felt for a pulse.

"She ain't got one anymore," Max told him.

The dwarf narrowed his eyes and slowly turned his head. "Max," the officer said, acknowledging him.

"Sarack," Max replied, "you haven't grown an inch since last I saw you."

"It's jokes like that, Max, old pal, that come up short," Sarack replied and then laughed.

Max chuckled, though his heart was heavy.

Sarack ordered his men to push back the gathering looky-loos. He walked over to where Max stood and pulled out a pack of Ogre Breath smokes. He took one out, put it in his mouth, and then fished out a packet of matches. "Just another day in New Gate," he said as he lit it.

"Goblin Town, you mean," Max corrected. He drew in the smoke from his pipe and let it stream out between his lips.

Snow began to fall. "Ya...Goblin Town. Mobs, whores, and junkies." Sarack rubbed his palms over his jacket, dusting off the snow that was clinging to it. "Poor girl. Did you know her, Max?"

Max considered his answer. "Tararill. She worked the streets around here. Sweet kid. I knew her, but not like that."

"Ya...Tararill." Sarack scratched his chin under his nearly body-length beard. "I put the arm on her a few times. Seemed like a smart girl. Never understood why she did the work."

"She belonged to the Mhi'ro mob. It wasn't really a choice for her. You know how that goes. You shorties got mobs where you come from, don't you?" Max asked.

"Shorties? Do you know what we call your type? Longshank Charley," Sarack retorted.

"Doesn't seem so bad." Max ran his fingers through his dark black hair.

Sarack thought on this. "Well, it is. Take it from me. If you were a dwarf, being called a Longshank Charley is about as bad as it gets."

Max nodded, conceding the issue. "If you say so." He put his hat back on.

"Jonstone is on his way. He made detective. I get the feeling he doesn't like you much," Sarack stated.

"He's a detective now? He was such a laxmore," Max replied. "Of all the assholes to get promoted, they had to promote that guy?"

Sarack chuckled. "Ya, I know what you mean." He walked over to where Tararill was lying. Her pinfeathers were still vibrant, but her skin was a haunting ice-blue now, and her body floated in a sea of crimson snow.

Taking a small pad out of his jacket pocket, Sarack said, "You better tell me what you saw, and don't leave anything out. Jonstone has his ways of finding out the truth in these matters."

Max tapped out the ash from his pipe and put it away. Then, he took a handful of snow and tried to clean the frozen blood off his hands by rubbing them together. Once done, he dried his hands on his pants and stuck them into the pockets of his wool overcoat.

"I was coming out of my office." He pointed across the street. "I heard a couple of pops. When I got up—"

"Up?" Sarack asked.

"Ya. I didn't want to get my head blown off, so I dove behind that cart over there."

"Okay." Sarack chuckled as he wrote down the account. "Then what?"

"I ran across the street and found Tararill lying just like you see her. I opened her coat and found the wound and tried to stem the bleeding, but...I couldn't stop it. I yelled for help and told the first person I saw to fetch the ambulance and the bronze. She died before she could say anything."

"Bronze? Max, you used to be a bronze. You should have a little more respect for us. We're just doing our job like everyone else. Not all of us can leave the force and start out as a private detective," Sarack said.

"I didn't so much leave as was forced to leave. Anyway, at least I don't have the city fathers dictating how I do my job now," Max stated with a shrug.

From down the street, the churning sound of an approaching steam carriage could be heard. It stopped a few yards away, and a blast of white mist burst from the pressure-release valve. A tall elf in a dark blue overcoat stepped out. He adjusted his rumpled Croquor hat and tilted it forward, making it a little crooked on his brow.

"Max," Jonstone said, "why are you here?"

"Luck," Max said with a crooked smile. "How's tricks, Nick?"

"Bad!" Jonstone looked over at Sarack. "Any valuable information?"

"Max gave me a statement. But it's not much."

Jonstone turned then stopped in his tracks as his eyes fell on Tararill. "Fathers of Old!" escaped his lips. "Sarack, get a blanket out of the car and cover her." He turned back to Max. "So, what haven't you told the sergeant?"

Max's eyes narrowed. Of all the years he'd known Jonstone, he'd never seen him taken aback like that. And they had both seen some terrible things while working in the heart of Goblin Town.

"I take it you knew her?" Max asked as he clasped his hands together and rubbed them furiously together.

"Of a sort," Jonstone replied.

"Like I told short stack, I came out of my office and heard someone fire a gun. When I came up, I saw the girl lying here. I tried to save her, but the bleeding was too much, and she died." Emotion was crawling up his throat. He stamped his feet one more time.

"Okay. You can go for now. Don't leave town," Jonstone said.

"If you need to find me, I'll be down at the Faye Café grabbing some grub." Max fished his gloves out of his pocket and put them on, then turned and started walking.

The area around the murder scene was filled with footprints smashed into the snow by the bronze, gawkers, and ambulance crew.

"Good luck, old pal," Max said under his breath.

A little farther down the walkway, he noticed the impressions of the fleeing killer's shoes, still barely visible.

He followed the steps. As he approached the corner of the block, he stopped. A few drops of red were in the snow alongside the footprints. The prints left the cement walkway and entered the alley.

He looked back at Jonstone. The elf was facing away. The faint footprints next to Max's were nearly gone. The shooter had slipped into the side street.

Between the two buildings—one a tenement with a red brick façade and the other an old stone warehouse—the space kept the snow in perpetual shadow. The overhang of the two structures shielded the footprints, preventing them from being buried.

The prints were odd. One appeared relatively normal, while the other was malformed like the end of a crutch or cane.

Max came to a faded yellow door, the paint peeling from age and neglect. He grabbed the brass handle and gave it a twist. The door was locked. He put his shoulder against it, but it didn't budge. He went down on one knee and peered through the keyhole. Only darkness met his gaze.

He walked back to the street, stopped, and peeked around. Jonstone was giving orders and pointing at the body. . Max quickly stepped out onto the sidewalk and headed down 56th toward the café.

The eggs were scrambled well, and he had toast with several cups of dark hythana, or, as ex-military men called it, "skull rush." Both the food and stimulating beverage fortified Max. He stood and paid at the register. He then took his overcoat, hat, and scarf from the rack and headed out into the falling snow.

There was no wind—only the curtain of descending white flakes. Though he would never admit it to another living person, Max was grieving. He'd seen more death than most, but as he grew older, every death he came across hit him harder and harder. And since he knew Tararill, he was filled with both rage and crushing sadness.

Once back at his office, he dispensed with his overcoat, went over to the wet bar in the corner, and poured himself a glass of Whipet Gaile. He sat down at his desk, turned his chair, put his feet up on the sill, and looked through the frosted window at the street.

The drift was almost as high as his window. There was no movement out there, save for the occasional wandering soul braving the storm.

After a while, and at the expense of half the bottle of gaile, Max figured he was wasting his time being in the office and resolved to head home. He was halfway to the door when the vocalrelay rang.

He crossed the room and picked up the earpiece. "This is Max."

The voice on the other end seemed distant—like someone talking from the back of a tunnel.

"Max Draber? I'm Mrs. Limiric Tre'hu. I was wondering if you had a moment. I need to hire a private detective, and your name was given to me."

"Really? I mean, what's this about?" Max asked.

"I'd prefer to speak in person, if you don't mind. And somewhere other than your office," Limiric stated.

Max felt annoyed. He preferred to do the initial meet-and-greet in his office. "Okay. How about the Goblin, Drog, Sword, and Shield on 42nd Street?"

"That will do. Can you be there in an hour?"

"I'll be there. See you then," Max said and hung up.

The Goblin, Drog, Sword, and Shield had been there since the Second Age. Imbued with old magic, its exterior appeared as new and fresh as the day it was covered by the spell. The inside was classic—carved wood paneling, exposed roof beams, a large fireplace at one end, and a bar of polished wood. Along the street side, the wall was covered with stained glass windows.

But while the tavern had not changed a day since it had been erected, the neighborhood had. The founders called it "Commerce Lane" in the old days. The street was populated with investment and banking houses. Time, though, is not without a hint of irony, for the neighborhood fell into disrepair after the nobles rebelled and moved the financial district uptown. Abandoned by the rich, the area had been overtaken by slumlords, bandits, and gangsters.

Over time, the poor and dispossessed came to call the area home, and it would eventually come to be known by the locals as Goblin Town, a rough-and-tumble area populated by migrant ogres, goblins, gnomes, dwarves, and their families from all over the world.

Chi'ra stood behind the bar. He looked up and saw Max come in. "Pirett! Max the loner, the detective, the wanderer."

Max smiled. "Chi'ra, how is the brood?"

"Ravenous and numerous! What brings you into my tavern?"

"Client," Max replied.

"It must be a good day to discuss business." Chi'ra nodded toward a set of dark booths in the back. "The High-most wants to have a word with you."

Max followed Chi'ra's finger. In the back in a booth, an older goblin looked over. Max recognized the head of the local mob sitting bathed in the low glow of a pale-yellow light. Mhi'ro the Skullcrusher was a no-nonsense type of fellow. A goblin with stern eyes and iridescent red-blue scales along his face and neck, he was not a person to be on the wrong side of.

Max started heading over but stopped at the bodyguard named Pir'na.

The guard was almost as tall as Max. The rainbow colors of his scales glinted in the low light. "Max Draber," the muscular hobgoblin said with a hint of joy. "What brings you to see the boss?"

"By request of the ole frother. Hoping it's just saying hello and I don't find myself sold to some giants in Hartakland," Max stated.

Pir'na smiled at the thought. "Wait here. I'll let the High-most know you're here."

"Wait. He can easily see I'm here." Max frowned and shook his head. Those employed by the mobs were not very bright.

Pir'na approached the master goblin and whispered. Mhi'ro nodded, and the bodyguard returned.

"He'll see you."

"Thanks, Pir'na. May you one day be given a territory to run," Max said as he went over to the High-most and bowed slightly.

"Eminence of the Ro, Lord of the family of forty, he whose stubby fingers are in every pie."

"Are you trying to be an asshole?" Mhi'ro motioned for Max to sit opposite him in the booth. "I have trouble knowing when you are being sarcastic. I suggest you don't walk such a fine line when you are summoned to speak to me. Respect is everything, and if you don't think so, perhaps you'd like to spend a week working in a brothel in Hartakland."

"No need for that," Max said worried his levity might render him dead. "I certainly did not mean any offense."

Mhi'ro narrowed his eyes. "Well, at least you are not a bronze anymore. I like that you've come a little more to my side of the world."

"Well, let's not start fitting me with a crew collar quite yet," Max said. "What did you want to see me about?"

"I wanted to ask you if you knew anything about Tararill's death. She was murdered this morning off 56th." Mhi'ro sipped something from a tiny cup on the table. "You were there. I can't have a young girl killed in my territory. At least not a murder I did not authorize." Mhi'ro turned and shouted at his lieutenants. "Any word from the street on Tararill's killing?"

Mhi'ro's crew looked at one another. "No one knows nothing boss," one of the goblins stated.

Mhi'ro looked back at Max. "Not ordered by me or mine...and that means I have a problem." His eyes strayed down to the cup in front of him. "I did know the girl. A good worker. And I want to know who killed her."

"Not killed. She was murdered," Max corrected.

Mhi'ro's jaw tightened. He was a goblin not used to being corrected. "What is it you know, Max?"

"She said something to me that was strange. Something about seeing something. She said they killed her. I figured if anyone knew about anything, it would be you."

"Kind of you to say," Mhi'ro said.

"She gave me a paper with the word 'balls' written on it," Max said.

"Balls... And it has nothing to do with those obscene things your kind dangle so carelessly between your legs? After all, her profession..."

"I don't think so," Max said. "I think it was something else. Though she was dying at the time."

"A death voice is always highly unreliable. Her mind might have been between worlds. Did you think of that before bothering me about balls?"

Max smiled. "I did. But I have a feeling—"

"Isn't it your feelings that got you into trouble with the bronzies? Why you're now a freelancer? How's the shoe-leather business, by the way?"

Sitting back, Max frowned. "You don't pull your punches, do you?"

"It is the one who will be dead who fights with half intent," Mhi'ro said. "I will make further inquiries about town and see if there is any information to be had. And if I find you have been holding out on me—"

"I have not!" Max quickly cut in.

"Well, you know how upset it would make me. I just hope I don't have to have some of my boys ask you the hard way next time."

"No need for that." Max stood up.

"Not so fast," Mhi'ro said. "One deed done is half a deed met. You will do a favor for me."

Max sat back down. "Okay, what?"

"I want you to bring a package to my younger son, Lib'ro." Mhi'ro snapped his fingers, and from another booth came a stout goblin, his scales glinting green and red in the glow of the electric lights. He set down a small, wrapped box on the table. "I was going to send Pir'na, but since you have come, I want you to do it. Your friends in the constabulary will not likely bother you as they would Pir'na."

Max took the parcel and waited. Mhi'ro motioned for him to leave. "Be punctual. Lib'ro is waiting at the Marmont Grocery at the corner of 41st."

Max stood. Nodding as if answering a question no one else heard, he turned and went over to the bar. After ordering a drink, he found a booth far away from Mhi'ro and his goons and sat at the table. After a while, a female goblin came in.

Unlike male goblins, females had a covering of tiny feathers over their bodies. Her plumage was captivating, catching the light and reflecting dark blues, reds, and greens from atop her head and down her cheeks.

She looked about the room and then went to the bar, her short, flowing blue gossamer dress billowing out, exposing her long feathered legs as she glided by.

The barkeep pointed over at Max, and she approached.

"You're Max Draber?" she asked, no hint of a goblin accent in her speech.

"Yes. What can I do for you?"

"May I sit?"

"Please." Max stood and waited for her to get comfortable. He also sat. "What can I do to assist you?"

She regarded him, her golden sclera almost glowing in the dim light. Her black slit pupils were focused on him, extracting every essence of Max's character. "I am Mrs. Limiric Tre'hu. I knew Tararill; she was my niece. Detective Jonstone told me you were the one who discovered her as she lay dying."

"He's right. She was weak. Didn't say much."

"What did she say to you?"

Max felt a little uncomfortable. "Well, I don't think she was in her right mind."

"What did she say to you, Mr. Draber?"

"Well, it wasn't what she said exactly. It was something written on a piece of paper she had. It had the word 'balls' written on it," Max stated.

"Balls?" Limiric asked, confusion written across her face.

"She said they killed her because she saw something. Like I said, she was probably hallucinating or delusional."

"Tararill lived with my husband and I for a few years, until she became involved in using vexethelene. I know it is a medicine, but she was abusing it. It broke my heart to have to send her away, but she was stealing from us, and I could not have that. I'm sure you understand, Mr. Draber."

"Indeed, I do. Very sorry to hear. It must have been quite hard to do such a thing."

"It was a hard decision. She was like a daughter to us. Unfortunately, a year later, my husband died suddenly."

"I'm sorry to hear." Max nodded solemnly. He raised his hand. The barkeep sent a waitress over, and she took their order for drinks. "I'll have a Whipet Gaile—no ice—and the lady will have..."

"Blue Bark and fillee, shaken three times and poured into a chilled stem glass." She pulled out a gold case and opened it. "I hope you don't mind that I partake?" She took out a rolled smokable.

"Not at all," Max said. "As long as you grant me the same courtesy." He pulled out his pipe and stuffed it. He then removed his silver lighter and extended the flame to Limiric, who took a few puffs and sat back. Max then lit his own and drew in deeply until the contents of the bowl were bright red.

Limiric looked about casually and then focused on Max again. "There is another reason why I'm here. The constables said my husband killed himself, but I'm sure he did not. He was murdered, and I think it may have something to do with the death of my niece."

The waitress brought the drinks over and set them down on the polished wooden table.

"Anything else? Can I bring you the lunch or dinner menu?" the young goblin asked.

"Bring me a steak and finger fries. The lady will have..." Max motioned to Limiric.

"I'll have the slurry worms, and bring rysom crackers," Limiric stated.

"Very good," the waitress said and dashed off into the kitchen.

"The police ruled my husband's death a suicide. They refuse to listen to me," Limiric said, a modicum of disappointment in her voice. "I'm sure he was murdered. And now my niece."

"Why would someone murder your husband and niece?" Max sat forward.

"My husband worked for New Gate Power. In his spare time, he liked to collect artifacts. A few years ago, he took a trip to East Hurot. There was an archaeologist there that had some items for sale. All very normal and legal, he told me. But when my husband returned, he began acting odd...secretive. He'd leave at strange hours, move money around, and bring less-than-reputable people to our house."

"So, he was secretive. I'd be out of a job if husbands and wives didn't keep secrets." Max lifted his glass and took a sip.

"My husband was as loyal as the day is long," Limiric stated.

"Sorry—force of habit," Max told her. "Naturally suspicious."

"A week before Hemet died, he gave me an envelope to store in our bank strongbox. After he was gone, I went to retrieve the letter. On the way there, I noticed someone following me. I Instead went to the beauty parlor. The person waited outside for a while, then I lost sight of him. I went directly home and stayed there. That was just a few days ago."

"Did you call the police?"

"I did. They told me I was just being paranoid, but I wasn't."

Max sat back. "Doesn't surprise me."

"I'd like to hire you to find out who killed my husband, and my niece."

Max thought on this. "Okay. Come to my office, and I'll get you one of my standard contracts."

"But what of the person following me? They're still out there," Limiric said, alarmed.

"Don't worry about that crumple. After our meal, you leave ahead of me. Go toward my office. I'll handle your tail."

He wrote down his address on a napkin and handed it to Limiric.

Chapter 2

Doing the Dutchy Gibbon

MAX WATCHED FROM THE door as Limiric exited the restaurant. It was a sketchy neighborhood, but he felt she knew her way around.

She turned left and passed the large stained-glass windows along the walkway. From across the street, a person wearing a heavy woolen coat and hidden beneath a fur hat came from the alley and began to follow her.

This was the type of tail Max liked—not too experienced and not too bright. Max held the doorbell, slipped out, and eased the door closed. The tail was just reaching the end of the block.

Locals were now about, despite the biting chill, and the undulating throng surged and weaved along the boulevards and streets like a great living thing. Max mingled, keeping the fiend just within view.

Humans, goblins, elves, and dwarves all went about tending to their daily business. Even under this thick blanket of snow, Goblin Town was busy. Dwarf bankers, elvish craftsmen, and goblin construction workers made a tapestry of this section of the city. In the shadows were the clans—the gangs that managed the numbers, gambling, prostitution, and stolen property.

A steam cart rumbled to a halt and blew its loud whistle to clear the pedestrians who were crossing the intersection. Max's target was just about to turn down 56th Street, which was just becoming busy.

A private steam omnibus with its large single push wheel drove up the broad travel way, conveying paying passengers to their homes and businesses. The free trollies ran on tracks along the middle of the street. They moved slowly, blasting steam from their fittings as they churned out black smoke like an angry dragon. Passengers leapt on or off as the craft lumbered along.

Limiric left the street and went into the building where Max's office was located. The tail crossed the street and lurked in an alley. Max knew the backway to that alley and made straight for it.

Moving with the stealth of a hunter, Max crept forward, careful not to step on anything that might give him away. He was crouched, and the figure ahead was standing with his back to him.

The heavy coat undulated, and the person took a pipe out of their pocket, stuffed it, and lit it. The figure leaned against the stark red brick of the building, puffing away and not concerned about anyone coming up from behind.

Max was almost there; another few feet and he might put the arm on the guy. Then, from under the coat, a yellow barbed tail peeked out, dusted the snow back and forth, and then withdrew.

"Lazermore," Max said loudly.

The figure leapt up, turned, and stared at Max. "Max?"

Max slipped his hand into his pocket, felt for the pistol, and pointed the barrel within his coat at the creature. "You're tailing a woman."

"What business is it of yours what I'm doing?" Lazermore's hands drifted toward his own coat.

"Don't. I've got the drop on you." Max waggled the gun around in his coat pocket.

"So, you do. What of it?"

Max considered his next set of words carefully. "Look...you snoop, I snoop. We're a lot alike. But this woman you're snooping on happens to be with me. She is my client. If that sticks going down, we can take this to the council."

Lazermore stiffened a bit. "No need to reach out to them. I just got my license clean. What do you want?"

"You blow in the wind, and we can keep this between us. I don't even mind that you report what we've talked about to your client. By the way, who is that?" Max eyed Lazermore.

"None of your human-suffering business!" Lazermore snapped.

"Tell him or her to stay out of my business. If not, I'm taking you to the council, and we'll see where the vonk shits in the woods." Max took a couple of fast steps forward.

Lazermore stumbled back into the street, tripped, and fell into a snowbank. His hat flopped off, and his polished white horns shone brightly in the sun. His face was severe and leathery, and his aqua-blue eyes locked onto Max's as he stared with a burning rage.

"Beat it, Lazermore! Come back when you're not such an asshole." Max said, taking another step.

Lazermore shot to his feet, collected his hat, and rushed off down the street. He hailed a steam carriage, leapt in, and vanished in a cloud of steam and soot as the cart rushed off into the distance.

"What a moocher," Max said under his breath as he took his hand off his pistol and headed across the street to his office.

Once inside the building, Max saw Limiric waiting by the door with a rolled smoke between her fingers. She watched him as he entered.

"So, what was the hubbub?"

The corners of Max's mouth turned up slightly. "You were being tailed by a fella named Lazermore—a competitor of mine, though he practices more in the area of the Netherworld. So, you might be the subject of a Netherworlder or maybe a townie. He wouldn't tell, and I didn't beat it out of him."

"I'm glad you didn't resort to violence. It is so crude and sad when such things happen," Limiric said.

"Come on in," Max told her as he opened his office door and waited.

Limiric entered and sat in a chair opposite Max's large desk. She glanced about the joint, then brought up the rolled smoke and took a long drag. Sitting back and crossing her legs, she took a beat, then exhaled the pungent mist into the air.

"What do you think it means?" she asked.

"Tararill might have gotten herself into something big. What was she up to? I need to find out who saw her last," Max stated. "I'll see if she had a Jimmy last night."

"Terrible that word. I hate to think of what she was doing out there."

"I'll find out. Her street manager...I know her. I'll find out who she saw last." Max went to the filing cabinet and brought out several papers. "Here's my standard contract. Says I get two hundred crowns a day, plus expenses, and a bonus if I get results. Just sign it there and there."

Limiric signed the documents. Max took one and put it back in his cabinet. The second he gave to Limiric. "Your copy," he said.

"Thank you for taking me on as a client." Limiric stood up.

"Listen, keep an eye on your back. Someone is interested, and until we know who, you are at risk. Check into the Claremont Hotel on Rafferty and 22nd Street. Tell the clerk I sent you. He'll set you up in a safe room. Stay there until you hear from me. If you don't hear from me in a few days, contact the police again, let them know you hired me, and tell them that I'm probably dead." Max took out his pipe, stuffed it, and then lit it.

Limiric nodded. "Rafferty and 22nd. The Claremont Hotel."

"Exactly."

Max watched Limiric from his window as she hailed a steam carriage. Once she was down the road, he picked up his vocalrelay and called the Claremont to let them know she was coming. He then put on his overcoat, took up the parcel from Mhi'ro, and headed for the Marmont Grocery on 41st Street.

It was the typical scene—a group of well-dressed hobgoblins hobnobbing in front of the store. As Max walked up, they eyed him with suspicion. Without a word, he strolled into the store.

"Maxie Draber," said Pol'uk, the subchief of the clan, who was stocking a shelf. "What lowly task brings you to our humble abode?"

Max removed the parcel from under his coat and tossed it on the table. "For Lib'ro. Consider it an express delivery."

From inside came a taller-than-average goblin, his florescent scales cascading red, blue, and green in waves as he stepped into the light.

"You took long enough. Father sent a runner to acclaim your arrival...a few hours ago. I was beginning to think you had no respect for me...or us." He motioned to his often-violent brethren sitting at the tables by the front door.

Pol'uk's scales shivered making a buzzing sound. "There must be respect, for one to do business."

"Come on, Pol'uk. You know I don't even have respect for myself," Max stated.

The goblins burst into laughter. Lib'ro picked up the package and looked Max up and down with a hard eye.

"Seems every time I see you, Maxie, you look like shit, smell like booze, and have the heavy heart of a human without a lover." He looked at the package and hefted it a few times in his hand. "But Father says to give you a few drops of respect, though I don't know why. Nonetheless, unless you are buying some tholian steaks or brink sausages, fade off. You've done your shifty deed for the day."

Max nodded. "Not a worry, Lib'ro. Glad to do favors for your clan. Even when limp words from your narrow beak can't rumple my hide."

"One day my father will die. Then, I'll be the mastifio. Favors like you get from Mastifio Mhi'ro will dry up. Then you might end up in one of my famous sausages." Lib'ro motioned to some of the hanging meat in the window.

"Point taken," Max told Lib'ro. "You wouldn't want me to just lay down to your patter. That wouldn't be...manly. Anyway, I'm sure you wouldn't want to ruin your signature sausages with some rancid man meat."

Lib'ro chuckled. "Maybe so. If there were an award for someone crawling along a razor's edge and not chopped to pieces, you'd win. Now, make like a shadow at noon."

Max spun around and headed off toward the underground transit. The yawning mouth of the entrance led to stairs, and the noise of thousands of travelers coming and going flooded over him.

Max made his way through the throng until he was on the platform. The shrill whistle of the coming chain of cars echoed down the tunnel. On finding a spot where he could stand and wait, Max pulled his handkerchief up to his face; the heat and smell of the food vendors and all those people were always a jolt.

The carriages rattled to a halt, the doors along the sides slid open, and everyone began to push and filter in. Max rammed his way in and found a pole to hold on to, leaving the seats for those truly in need.

Out of the corner of his eye, he noticed an elf halfway down the car watching him. He wore ordinary working people's clothes, a knit hat, and fingerless gloves, but there was something not poor or working class about him.

Max looked up at the map on the upper wall of the car. He intended to get off on 13th to talk with an artifact specialist he knew from the old days. Ten stops to go.

The doors closed, and the cars rattled forward as the cable below the conveyance latched onto the carriages' underside and drew them toward their next stop. Great steam engines under the city drove the mechanical systems that drew underground carriages along, carried lifts skyward, and provided power to many of the city systems that ventilated and warmed the homes and offices.

Max glanced over; the elf was reading a newspaper. As the cars rounded a corner, the lights flickered on and off. He looked again, and the elf was a few seats closer now. They rolled into another station and came to a halt.

Nine more stops to make, Max thought. The elf glanced over and then back at his paper. The doors closed, and the vehicle was again in motion. This was repeated seven times. On the penultimate stop, Max garnered his strength. He didn't like being shadowed, and he needed to know whether it was real or his imagination. So, he waited for the doors to the car to open, and he started to count. It would be thirty seconds until they'd close again. At fifteen seconds, he quickly maneuvered to the doorway and stepped out.

Down the platform, the trailing elf popped out as a few travelers forced their way on. Max jumped back on. The elf did the same. The driver of the transport rang the bell, indicating the doors were closing. Max jumped back out and then back in.

The doors closed, and the elf was trapped on the platform as the carriages moved forward.

"Stop!" shouted the elf. "Open the doors!" He chased the cars as they plunged into the tunnel.

Max chuckled as he watched the darkness of the underway swallow the transport, and the lights inside came on. At least he was rid of one irritant. Clearly the fool wasn't experienced enough to know the Dutchy Gibbon maneuver. The Dutchy Gibbon – the third rule of snooping, to make one's pursuer reveal themselves by making them have to react fast. Max chuckled as he remembered the panicked expression of the tail's face as he yelled for the transport to halt.

How many more were lurking out there? And who was putting so much time and money into snooping around after his client? He was sure they wouldn't send so inexperienced a tracker to follow him again.

Chapter 3

A Salty Fellow

13TH STREET WAS BUSTLING. The Grover Lapis Building was five stories tall and had no elevator. The dwarf Max wanted to see, a purveyor of ancient and "magic" relics, was on the third floor. Frankly, Max did not give too much credence about such nonsense. Relics did exist, he'd learned about them in school, but they mostly seemed trivial, toys for amusement rather than something to help the common worker.

The filigree scribing on the door read, "William J. Bonerville, Esq. Rare Antique Dealer, Licensed." He grabbed the knob, pulled the door, and stepped inside.

A strong smell of lacquer, old leather, dust, and furniture polish rushed into his nostrils. The place was crammed with items, some still in crates and boxes. He walked down a narrow pathway to a wider area around a tall counter. He reached for the bell, and up popped William J. Bonerville.

"Well, as I live and breathe! Max Draber, private detective. What causes you to darken my doorway on this fine day?"

Max smiled and took off his hat. "Good to see you, Bill. How's tricks?"

"The romp is good, and the profit satisfactory. What can I interest you in? I have a box that tells your future. Or perhaps you'd like to purchase a pair of spectacles that allow you to see your opponent's cards? How about a flask that will change your gaile into wine...or is it the reverse?" He scratched his ample beard.

"No thanks, Bill. I'm actually here for your knowledge," Max said.

William swelled a bit with pride. "Really? You want my professional opinion on something?"

Max nodded.

"Can I get you a glass of something? I have a fine lummerum—very dark, with the wonderful hint of harrow wood and claption spice. Quite refreshing."

Max took out his pipe and lit it. "Sure, why not? Set it up, and I'll knock it back."

William produced a crystal decanter filled with a dark liquor. He poured two glasses and then sipped his. "Come on into my office, where we can speak freely. Moreish! Come watch the front!"

Another dwarf appeared, his long beard nearly tripping him as he approached. He grabbed a feather duster and began to dust the items around the counter.

William led Max along a winding path through the store to a back office. He sat behind a small, highly polished dark-wood desk and leaned forward, waiting for Max to ask his question.

"I won't beat about," Max began. "A client of mine had some info related to some sort of balls. I think they're antiques and worth some scratch."

William visibly blushed under his beard. "Balls," he repeated. "How delightful. You're asking me about balls!"

"Okay! Don't get all hully-bully about it. Do you know about some high-priced or special antique balls for sale in the collectors' world, or don't you?" Max pressed.

"Look, Max, I know you're not a believer in the old stuff—powerful magic, I mean. But there are all manner of items circulating from the far west and the south that the rich and mighty would like to possess. Much of it comes from old tombs or burial grounds, and some from archaeological digs. Most are fakes made to look or seem like real magic items. But sometimes we see something legendary or mythological. Few ever surface and make a row among my brethren. Once such an item or items are found, someone will reach out to me or one of my colleagues, and it gets bought up quick."

"What about the balls?" Max asked.

"Could be the mummified testicles of King Lubin the Third." William chuckled. "Poor fellow lost them when the royal burial priests removed them and put them in a jar like his other organs. Worth some Royal Bills, but not particularly worth stealing." He thought for a moment. "Might be the magic scepter of Lord Roll, the ogre baron who ruled the lands of Trud. It had three orbs of light that sat on the end. But no one really knows what good it was. No records are known to exist that describe what it did, other than look lovely. Then there are the floating balls of Turin." William pulled over a leather-bound book on his desk and opened it. "Here it is—the

Lords of Turin ordered the shire mages to create the Moderan. The plans called for it to stand two hundred feet tall. It would house one hundred warriors. Inside, it had a never-ending food source, waste facilities, sleeping and recreation rooms, and, most of all, a long-lasting power source. It says that the Turin Balls were created to power the Moderan and make it run forever."

Max sat back and puffed on his pipe. "I see the interest."

"It is said that the Moderan was dismantled two thousand years ago. The parts were either melted down, repurposed, or sent to far-flung places about the world." William looked at the book again. "As a power source, if it runs off magic, it could make someone quite a lot of scratch. What exactly did your lady friend say?" William's eyes grew wide with interest.

"She said, 'They killed me for it.' Then she died."

"How dreadful!" William blurted. "Wait! She was murdered?"

"Yes."

"What a horrible thing." William consumed his drink. "She told you this as she lay dying?"

Max took a puff and then a drink. "Not exactly. She had a paper scrap with some info on it."

"What did it say?"

Max finished his libation. "'Balls. Fifteen hundred hours. Bring your bid.' Sounds an awful lot like some sort of auction."

"That could refer to anything. But if people are killing one another for it, it sounds big, and nothing is as big as the energy source the Turin Balls could provide."

"Look, Bill, keep an ear to the ground on this one. If you hear anything about those balls, let me know." Max slid the glass across the desk and stood up. "Thanks for the drink. Next time, just make it gaile."

"Gaile? How foul! You are a barbarian, Max Draber!" William scolded.

Max headed toward the door. William followed.

"I'll be sure to tell you." William grabbed Max's pant leg. "Listen, if it is..." He looked over both shoulders. "There are those who stand to make a fortune in the power industries, and I'm sure they will stop at nothing to acquire it to exploit its power or learn how it works. Try not to take any crazy chances, Max. I've grown fond of you and would hate to lose such a good...friend."

Max pulled his pant leg away. "You know me, Bill... No more chances than I have to." He stepped through the door and headed down the stairs.

Max hailed a steam carriage and headed to the Heartwood Tavern on Lumbarg Street and 42nd. The late afternoon was growing older by the minute, and he needed a stiff one before heading home. He paid the driver and watched the carriage steam away into traffic.

Just a couple glasses of aged gaile to help get me into a fit sleep. That's all, Max told himself.

He pulled open the door and strolled in. The place was old—at least 500 years. Frosted glass windows let in the light from the street, and polished brass railings ran the length of the bar. Leather stools were supported on brass poles, which were secured to the floor with long bolts to prevent anyone from using one as a weapon if a fight commenced.

"Max!" called Huggley from behind the bar. His loose-fitting shirt, secured just at the biceps with black garters, was draped over his ample ogre frame. "What'll it be?"

"The usual. And don't try and foist any that rot-gut on me...the good stuff from around back," Max said quietly to the looming barkeep.

Huggley smiled and chuckled. "Max, you are always suspicious. I guess your type of work suits you right down to the ground." He pulled a bottle from under the bar, removed the cork, and poured some into a glass. "Here ya go. The good stuff, as requested."

"Got any chookle?" Max asked.

Huggley looked about the bar, and then from his apron he produced a bar of a dark waxy substance and set it next to Max's glass. "A roy bill and four stones for both."

Max took out his wallet, handed the ogre the money, and then fished around in his pocket for the metal disks. Huggley nodded and then went down the bar, asking if anyone needed a refresher.

After taking a bite out of the chookle, Max took his snack and drink and found a booth in the back. He sat there sipping his gaile and waiting for the creamy chookle to trick his brain into forgetting Goblin Town and his troubles. It didn't take long.

At first, the lights in the bar became vibrant, but soft around the edges, enveloping the surroundings in a warm glow. Then, the other lights—the ones made of electrified gas-colored pink, red, purple—all pulsed and began to swallow all who sat too close to them.

Deep within Max, he felt the gnawing of his past—not the serene flight he'd hoped would separate him from his reality. The war, the killing, the many sacrifices...it all welled up.

It started as a small matter. A rebellion in the troll lands. It drew in the elves of Nord, then the dwarves of Hillfort. A rally cry for men from Argos and other countries was made. Max volunteered. It took two weeks on a steamer to reach the fighting.

The elves had made trenches, zig-zagging through the fields and countryside. On the other side, swarthy elves, three toed trolls, tickertok gnomes, and the blue skinned humans from Cree waited.

He ran from crater to crater, avoiding the rapid popping from the clockwork guns spitting gold projectiles from their peroxide-powered rounds.

On turning his head, he saw Vieger—in his hand, a tosser bomb. Vieger hefted it over the lip of the trench, and they both heard the explosion and then the screams of the enemy on the other side.

Max's heart felt impaled, and pain filled his every vein. Both of his friends died that day in the trenches when the enemy assaulted the wasteland. Snag wire, pain holes, and gun swords were all covered in blood, as the bodies piled up like cordwood.

He took up his drink and swallowed the contents. Huggley was at the far end of the bar.

A voice of someone nearby melded with the noise of the patrons: "Yan herosh!"

Max's mind drifted. He was still on the dirty ditch. Bullets were flying over his head. There was there—the enemy soldier—clambering over the edge of the trench. Max was outside his body. He saw himself raise his rifle and fire directly into the other's face. The shot took away half his skull. It was a legal shot in the heat of battle. The enemy elf staggered back and then came at Max, grabbing him around the neck. He was choking him in the last few seconds of life. Max fell back, the fingers tight around his throat. He couldn't breathe; the hands were like vises. The body became limp and fell to the side. Max was alone and alive, for the sake of the gods!

Huggley poked at Max's shoulder. "You still in there?"

"Herosh..." Max mumbled.

"Surrender? Who in the name of Rike are you surrendering too, Max?"

Hands grasped at Max's shoulders. He was flying and then landing over something. Was it a sky bomb? Was this it? Would he finally pay the price for the murder he'd committed? Join his friends in the afterlife?

Max struggled to a sitting position—head pounding, mouth dry, eyes in agony. He stumbled to the lavatory, turned on the water, and filled the basin.

Splashing the ice-cold liquid over his face and head, he looked up into the mirror. The lines on his face were deeper than they'd ever been. How many years had passed since the war? He made a wobbly trek back to bed and put on his shirt. Who'd undressed him? Someone must have carried him to his flat.

On went his pants, shoes, vest, and jacket. He needed some breakfast and a hot cup of skull rush. He slipped on his overcoat—the pistol was still in the pocket—and made for the stairs.

He left his building and headed out onto the street. The light outside was harsh. No clouds obscured the rising sun; its heat warmed the land and melted the snow, making a mess of the streets and walkways. He hailed a steam carriage.

"Take me to Claremont Hotel on Rafferty and 22nd," he requested.

The driver eased the vehicle out into traffic, blew the steam whistle to warn all around, and increased speed down the street. It took a few minutes, but the carriage turned onto 22nd Street and headed south to Rafferty and the fifteen-story red-stone Claremont.

"Thanks." Max gave the driver a few stones for his trouble.

"Sir," the driver said, "there is a Paddington Reaver that's been following us since I picked you up. Just thought you'd like to know."

Max smiled. "I know, and thanks for the warning." He tossed the fellow another stone.

The carriage pulled out into traffic, blasting the whistle and narrowly missing half a dozen pedestrians, who flung themselves out of the way.

"Stay on the walkways!" shouted the driver as he sped off, looking for another fare.

The Claremont was one of the newer and fancier multistory inns dominating the skyline just adjacent to Middle Park. Over the last couple of decades, the park had become the centerpiece of bustling moneymaking tourism. Investors realized this and bought up the old manor houses that had once circled the parklands, tearing them down and building gleaming and somewhat gawdy edifices in their place to fleece travelers of their royal bills and silver stones.

Glowing pink and red flashing letters spelled out "Claremont Inn" fed by cheap and plentiful electricity that illuminated the wet walkway and Max. When it had opened, he'd been there to see what all the hype had been about. It was spectacular, with all the gaming tables just inside, craft-deco artwork with gold and brass, and gleaming sculptures of colored glass—light and shadow. Max felt it was like getting clubbed in the head with a truncheon made of pixy dust while loaded on gaile and chookle. But was it a cultural triumph to the creative spirit? He wasn't sure.

"Well, Max, how in the name of Cinder are you?" Carlum Hundley asked as Max approached the counter.

"What do you hear, Carlum? How's tricks?" Max smiled and put his elbows on the counter. "Our guest...I need to see her."

"Not a problem." Carlum retrieved a key and motioned for Max to follow behind the counter.

They retreated into the back office. Carlum used the key to open a secret door that allowed access to a warren of corridors. They turned left, then right, and then went up some stairs.

"Here," Carlum said as he opened a door.

Inside was another hallway, but it was not pragmatic; it was ornate with lush carpet and fine-finished wall sconces made to look like roaring flames of orange and red.

"Where are we?" Max asked.

"Second floor, halfway down the hall not far from our elevator. Maintenance hallways can serve several purposes," Carlum said.

They walked down the corridor. Carlum stopped at a door marked 263 and knocked.

The door handle turned, and there stood Limiric in a long housecoat and fuzzy slippers. "Max." She smiled. "Do come in."

"Thanks, Carlum. I owe you a few favors for this one," Max said.

Carlum chuckled and then became serious. "She'll be safe here for as long as you need."

Max nodded. Carlum left and closed the door.

"Did you find out anything?" Limiric asked.

"Not much, I'm afraid. But those who might have killed your husband and your niece...they will reveal themselves—especially if they think you know about what they're looking for."

Max took out his pipe and lit it. He walked over to the narrow arrow-slit window and peered out. Down on the street, a black Paddington passed and then stopped. A figure got out of the passenger side and rushed into the inn. Though he wore a hat, it was obvious he was a tall elf.

"What is it?" Limiric asked.

"It appears they do think you know something. Come with me," Max told her and opened the door.

He led her down the hallway to a T intersection and pushed her a little way along the left passage. He put his finger to his lips, and with his right hand, he pulled the pistol from his pocket and waited.

A few minutes passed in silence, and then from down the passage, he heard voices. Carlum was babbling rather loudly. Max figured he was trying to warn them.

"I don't know what you think you'll find here!" Carlum blurted.

"Shut up and show me the door," said a voice with a southern elf accent.

"Okay. You don't need that. All it is, is a storage room for building maintenance." Carlum's voice was getting closer. "All you had to do was ask to see it. You didn't need to throw that bird leg in my face."

Max heard a key in a lock, followed by the sound of a door handle clicking. He counted to four and then peeked around the corner. The hallway was clear.

"Stay here," Max said to Limiric.

"Watch yourself," Limiric whispered.

Max nodded, then quickly moved to the doorway and waited. From inside the room, Max heard Carlum say, "I don't know any girl—goblin or other!"

The sound of a struggle erupted. Pistol in hand, Max threw the door open and rushed in. He caught the elf with his back to the door.

Max brought the barrel of his weapon down onto the hatted head of the tough, felling him in one go. The elf collapsed unconscious into a heap on the floor. Carlum stood in stunned shock, blood dripping from his fat lip.

Without a word, Max ransacked the elf's clothing, pulling out his leather billfold, a handful of porcelain peroxide shells, a small hand tablet, a few silver stones, and some papers wrapped in a handkerchief. The ID in the envelope described the hoodlum as Farlung Hardrain, residence 124 Dragon Scale Street, Hobart City.

"Grab his feet!" Max barked. "Let's get this stink hole downstairs. Once we're in your office, call the constables and ask for Detective Jonstone. Tell him this thug tried to strong-arm you for cash. You struggled with him, and he fell and bumped his head." Max pocketed the elf's pistol and shells.

As Max backed out into the hallway, he saw Limiric down the hall. In her eyes was fear.

"Stay there. I'll be back for you in a few minutes. Got to help Carlum take out the trash."

Limiric nodded and hid around the corner. Max and Carlum hauled the elf to the main office and trussed him up with some rope.

A groan escaped the lips of the unconscious elf. Max looked over the papers wrapped in the cloth. The fellow's real identification card was one of them.

"Ah! He's a contractor. Here's his actual name. Oswald Wardrum, 116 years old. He's from New Fleet Raven's Look. Southern all the way." Max looked over at Carlum, who was on the blower with the constables.

On hanging up the mouthpiece, Carlum gingerly touched his lip. "Guy packed a hell of a punch," he said. "The constables will be here in a few minutes."

"Just enough time to slip out the back," Max told him. "Remember: neither I nor Limiric were here. The guy just came in demanding money. That should put him up at the slog for a few days at least."

Carlum pressed a button, and a staff member appeared at the door. "Fetch me some ice and a towel. And bring me some gaile." The young man dashed off. Carlum looked at Max. "For the lip." He walked over to the trussed-up elf and belted him in the face. He then turned, went over, and sat behind his desk.

Max opened the door, looked back, and said, "You got even. Leave it at that."

Carlum looked annoyed but nodded. "I think I got what I wanted."

"Good. You're a good man, Carlum. No point slumming it in the weeds with the rokers." Max entered the corridor and closed the door behind him.

A few minutes later, he and Limiric were on the street. Max grabbed a steam carriage, and they headed for the northwest of the city—the Sutro Borough, which was not far from the Surgy City Bridge. Max had a lawyer friend who owed him a favor, and he had a place he seldom used up along the south coast just outside Surgy City.

Chapter 4

Just the Skinny

IT WAS A WHOLE DIFFERENT scene across the bridge in Surgy City. No sky-climbing buildings, no cramped streets with wall-to-wall people, and no steam carriages competing for space. It was spread out—homes on lots, villas along the riverfronts, and quaint country stores and shops.

Max felt exposed—in the line of fire—there. It was too much like the lands and towns he'd wandered during the war.

Surgy City straddled the Ingrid Canal, one of the original trade network canals that made the commerce barons of the old noble order so wealthy. Those water lanes created the cities on the islands and laid the groundwork for the modern world.

Limiric and Max booked a private car for the steam coach ride across the bridge to the mainland. It took thirty minutes to reach the Neptal Station in Surgy and just a few minutes more to get the southbound coach to Waverly Station in Limpet Town, halfway between Surgy and Freetown.

From Limpet, Max rented a steam carriage that took them out to Sinclair Beach and all the large homes built for the rich and famous who lived in the five boroughs and beyond.

Once they were inside the multistory villa, Max took Limiric downstairs to the safety vault. The entrance was hidden, and it took two keys to open it from the outside. However, from the inside, it took only the press of a button to allow access.

"You'll be safe here for sure. Stay in the vault. It has its own kitchen, bedrooms, and a larder with plenty of food. There is some booze in the bar, and all the news of the day comes across the crier tape connected to this wall. Just flip this switch," Max told her. "I have to go back to the city. If you need to reach me, use the wire on the wall. It connects to the sorter in Limpet. Ask her to connect you to my number in Sutro."

Max turned to go, but Limiric grabbed him by the arm. She was trembling. "Do you have to go so soon?" she asked.

Max looked down into her spectacular eyes. There was a scent in the air that stimulated his libido. She was wearing her margowa musk, a powerful stimulant that affected both goblin and human.

Her soft, feathery lips were turning a darker shade of red. She stroked his arm, and he fought the desire to pull her in and kiss her.

"I hope we can commit our passion soon. I am not opposed to doing tracea with you. I am open, as I think you are," Limiric told Max.

He pulled away gently. His heart was racing and his mouth dry. "Not...now. Those looking for you have it in their minds to ask you the hard way for any link to the treasure they seek. I don't want that to happen, and I know you don't." He stepped back toward the vault door. "When I find out what's going on and stop them, then we can explore what this is."

The corners of her mouth drooped down as she sat on a plush leather chair. "Then go!" she abruptly said. But just as quickly, her mood softened. "Yes, it is for the best. If there is fire in us after, we can commence honestly and not with clouded minds."

Max saw a slight smile form on her lips. The tips of the small feathers covering her head twitched. He backed out the door and closed the vault. Now, he was off to the city to find some answers.

The ride back on the steam coach was uneventful. He kept an eye out for any suspicious characters but saw none. Once back in Sutro, he disembarked and caught a carriage to the 20th Precinct. Sergeant Jack Ironhammer was manning the front desk.

"By the mercy!" Jack blurted. "Max Draber. Detective Jonstone has been looking for you, Max."

Max nodded. "I figured that would be the case. I'm here now. Why don't you give him a ring and tell him?"

Jack picked up the receiver and flipped the switches to Jonstone's office. "Detective? It's Jack at the front. I have Max Draber here asking for you... Okay." Jack looked over at Max. "He said for you not to move. He's on his way down."

Jonstone came down the stairs. "Max...with me."

After following the detective to a room off the main hallway, Max pulled out one of the brown wooden chairs, sat down, and took out his pipe.

"So, Max, what do you know?" Jonstone asked.

"What do you know about an Oswald Wardrum?" Max asked.

Jonstone sat back and crossed his legs. "I might know about him. A hired tough. Does work for the various mobs in the city." He leaned forward. "Is he involved in the murder of Ms. Tararill?" He removed a smoke, put it into his mouth, and lit it with a match from his desk.

Max puffed his pipe. "He tried to put the arm on a friend of mine. At least that's what we told your friends at the 12th." Max chuckled. "The bastard was tailing me. He's mixed up in this right up to his chin. If you leave now, you'll see him over at the 12th since he's being collected at the Claremont Hotel."

"You got your round ear to the hard ground today, don't you, Max? What were you doing at the Claremont Hotel?" Jonstone asked.

Shrugging, Max blew a smoke ring across the desk and smiled. "Have you heard about any cock brows in the city?"

"Like?"

"Big antiquity buyers or powerful politicians... You know...oddities showing up?" Max asked.

"I've read the sheets. There's a human fellow named Pornet Lewis—a puff-pocket from the mainland who's here at a conference for inventors. But that's outside Goblin Town. He's staying in a villa on the west side of the park. There's an elf lady named Silimet Noland. She's over at the Hilltop Inn on the east side of the park. Then, there is a gnome fellow—a shifty gaslight sort—working for a big electric company on the mainland. I don't know where he's staying."

"Wow. Short list."

"I like the list when it's short," Jonstone replied. "So, out with it. What have you got on the Tararill case?"

"Look, Nick, I have a few irons in the fire, but nothing ready to spill yet. I want to find the fiend who did this as much as you—maybe more. Just don't crowd me. You know I have much more latitude to work than you do. I'll get some results...and soon."

"How does Mrs. Limiric Tre'hu fit into this?" Jonstone asked.

"She's the victim's aunt." Max eyed Jonstone for a moment. "You know that. Why are you shaking me down?"

"Just making sure you're being straight with me. You know the third rule of constable work."

"Ya. Never ask a question you don't know the answer to."

"Don't hold out on me, Max. And that's an official warning."

"I got the message, Nick." Max got up and headed for the door.

Max hailed a steam carriage and headed down to 56th Street. There, he got out at his office but then crossed the street. He stood for a minute where Tararill had fallen, and then he looked back across the street at his office.

"She was coming to see me," Max said aloud. He turned and headed to the building where he'd found the yellow door.

On trying the handle, he found that it was still locked. So, he headed around to the front of the looming structure. There was a grocery on the bottom floor and apartments on top. He entered the Gol'thu Grocery.

"Hello, Max," said Gol'thu, the proprietor. "Looking for some mammal lactate? I have some fresh from Lector Farms."

"Not here for food. You have a yellow door in the alley. Do you know what it leads to?"

"I think it goes to the steam tunnels under the building. There is access through here." Gol'thu grabbed an electric torch and led the way into the back of the store and down a flight of stairs.

At the bottom was a hallway that bifurcated—one leading farther under the structure, and the other leading to the yellow door.

Naked bulbs illuminated the passage in a dull yellow light. Max got down on one knee to examined the floor.

"Hand me that light," Max requested. Gol'thu complied.

The faint outline of a boot sole was clear. Next to it was a strange, small, circular pattern.

"A peg leg," Max said.

"Pardon?" Gol'thu asked.

"Not you, Gol'thu. The last person to come through here has one good foot and a peg for the other." Max turned and began to move farther under the building, following the tracks and a host of steaming-hot pipes.

Gol'thu stopped. "I need to go back to my store. The street scamps have probably picked me clean by now."

"Don't fret. I'm a big boy. You get back. I'll be okay."

Gol'thu turned and headed in the opposite direction. Max pursued the odd footprints.

Max slowly made his way through a maze of tunnels and then stopped as the impressions on the cement floor dried up. Shining his torch around, he saw a set of stairs not far off.

Some treads went up, and some went down. Max looked below: a soft glow from some electric wall blister lights highlighted the metal steps.

Max shrugged, felt for the pistol in his pocket, and headed downward. With each footfall, the metal stairs rattled and creaked. As he made the landing, he looked through the wrought iron balusters onto the next floor. No light was visible, except for his own. He moved down cautiously.

Once he reached the next level, he flashed his light around. Stretched out in front was a long hallway with some openings on either side and darkness further on.

As he took a step a flash lit up the stairwell and tunnel. Max spun around, pulling his gun from his pocket. Standing there was a figure lighting a smoke.

"Lazermore," Max said.

"Draber." Lazermore drew in the acrid smoke and spewed it out again. "No need for the popper." He pointed at the pistol. "I know we ain't been chummy, but no need this time for bruiser behavior. We ain't chummy rollies or muscle boppers."

Max lowered his peroxide piece. "What brings you here?"

"Same as you. One very expensive stolen item."

"You looking to steal it?" Max asked.

"No, Maxie. You got it all wrong. I'm here like you—on official business. The Updike, Hallion, and Pickersleve insurance company hired me. They're very interested in recovering... Well, you know by now, I'm sure." His long yellow tail swung back and forth.

Max shined the torch in Lazermore's green and red eyes. "You mean the balls."

"Of course." Lazermore remained leaning against the wall. He put his smoke between his leathery lips, drew in, and then exhaled toward Max. "So, Maxie, I told them of your involvement." He chuckled. "Our little encounter in the snow the other day. I suggested that I reach out to you at some point with a proposition."

"What proposition? Don't think I've forgotten about the Dunwick incident and all the heat I took because you buggered off, leaving me holding the bag."

"Everyone makes mistakes, Maxie boy. It's a condition easy to get in to. After all, it is Goblin Town. But this is on the ups. Come to the Baxter Building on 40th. Third floor, suite 315. Try to be there in an hour." Lazermore stepped forward and tossed the stub of his smoke on the ground. He climbed onto the first step. "To show you I'm of good faith, the tracks lead to a hoard of loot a few rooms down. Not sure if any of it is legal or stolen—not really my business. But the balls weren't there." He walked up the remainder of the steps. "See you in an hour, Maxie. Don't keep my clients waiting."

Max legged it down the passage and looked in each room. As Lazermore had said, one room was filled with all manner of items.

"Well, that horned daemon bastard!" Max swore.

He searched the room—every tin, box, crate, and bag. Nothing ball-like was at hand.

What was the one-legged killer doing here? Max thought. Then, he saw it. It was sitting on a shelf along one wall in plain view. An antique pistol—a scrolled brass barrel, carved wooden body, and staghorn inlaid grip.

He walked over to it, took out his handkerchief, and used it to pick up the weapon. The pistol had been recently discharged and the breach was discolored. It was clear that the killer had been careless in sealing it. The pinhole had delivered the rod of manganese dioxide into the chamber, but the blast of steam had backfired up through the breach lock. It was a particular failing of the ancient weapon. The killer most likely got scalded a bit. Max would keep an eye out for a one-legged assailant with some facial or hand burns. He put the weapon back down.

The torch was beginning to grow dim, gobbling up the electricity in the power cells. Max made his way back to the grocery store. He checked his watch and saw that he had twenty minutes to make it over to 40th.

The steam carriage dropped Max off in front of the Baxter Building. He entered through the revolving glass door and stopped at the marble wall displaying the occupants: "3rd floor—Updike, Hallion, and Pickersleve Insurance Provider."

He took the lift to the third floor. Upon exiting, he approached a reception desk with a no-nonsense, unhappy-looking orc sitting behind it.

"What can I do for you?" the orc asked.

"I'm Max Draber. I'm here at the invitation of the partners."

"I'll ring that you are here. Please take a seat." The orc pointed at a set of couches and chairs formed into a square around a central cocktail table.

A few moments passed, and Lazermore approached. "Ready, Maxie boy? Come on in." He led the way to a conference room down a busy hallway.

Upon entering, Max was struck by the odd conference table and setting. The table was angled with an elevated end tapering down to a low end. He was led to the lower end and sat in a seat that was nearly as low as the floor. A moment later, in walked the partners of the firm.

The gnome, who was smartly dressed and wearing a top hat, went directly opposite Max and climbed up onto a chair that elevated him well above everyone else. He looked down at Max and waited.

Two dwarves followed and took up seats on either side of the table closest to the gnome. Several others came in: a human woman, a female elf, and two large goblins. All of them had a higher sitting position than Max.

Lazermore remained standing, leaning against the wall with a smoke between his lips and his tail swishing back and forth.

"Mister Draber? We are eager to hear what you have found out regarding the two murders and the missing item we seek," the gnome stated.

"That's funny. I don't seem to have your contract in front of me. When did you hire me? I'm sure my fee was quite outrageous." Max removed his pipe and struck a match.

"We don't allow smoking in here, Mister Draber!" one of the dwarves said sternly.

Max looked over at Lazermore, who shrugged and kept smoking.

"Let me be clear," Max began. "My client is the one I report to—not this circus. If you want me to help you with something, come by my office and sign a contract. If not, you'd better start telling me how this benefits me and my client."

The gnome looked annoyed. "You are a pip, Mister Draber. We have a common desire—to find the antiquity that has been stolen. You see, we're an insurance department and like to keep our money. We do not like to pay money for items stolen if the items can be retrieved." He pointed at Lazermore. "We've employed this investigator to help locate our property. Now you, another investigator, are involved, and we would just like to form a common alliance to recover our lost item."

"Who is the insured?" Max asked.

"Mister Draber, it would be irresponsible of me to tell you at this early stage. We have a contract to offer you. It protects us and you as we work together." The gnome nodded, and the human female brought a stack of papers and pen.

She placed the papers on the table, but they slid back toward Max. He put his hand on them to hold them there. Flipping the papers with his thumb, he looked back at the gnome. "And you want me to sign this monstrosity now?"

"If it isn't too much trouble," the gnome replied.

"Trouble?" Max looked around the room. "I'll have my attorney look it over. If it truly is reasonable, I'll be happy to put in with you. If it's even a tiny bit crap, you can all go jam a ratikin up your collective asses." Max stood up.

"We wouldn't want it any other way. Get back to us by tomorrow. Lazermore will walk you out." The gnome climbed down from his perch and led the others out the door.

Lazermore chuckled. "Maxie, you are one unbendable sod."

Max nodded. "Got to be in this business, or chumps like them take meeps like us for a ride."

"Follow." Lazermore led the way downstairs to the lobby. "Look, Maxie, these guys upstairs mean business. Don't cross 'em. If you do, they might ask me to fix it. I don't want to have to do that." He turned and headed to the lift. A moment later, Lazermore was gone.

Max headed out and caught a steam carriage that took him to his office. He picked up the vocalrelay and rang his attorney. The dwarf rushed over to Max's office.

"What you got for me Max?" Lennard Buckler asked as he came through the door.

Max tossed the papers on the desk. "Give these the once-over, if you don't mind. Be quick about it. I have to give these guys an answer by tomorrow."

Lennard picked up the document and put it into a leather case he carried. "Will do. I'll have it back in the hour." He turned and left.

Max fished out a bottle of gaile, poured himself a glass, and sipped it. He then grabbed the receiver of the vocalrelay and dialed the constables.

"Hey, it's Max. Let Jonstone know to check out the tunnels under Gol'thu Grocery. There's a room down there with a bunch of pinched items. One, I think, is the murder weapon." He hung up and put his feet up on the desk. Just as he lifted the glass to his lips, his door came crashing in.

Chapter 5

Never Pull the Ears of a Dragon

MAX SHOT TO HIS FEET as three six-foot-tall, thickly muscled orcs strolled in.

"I hear things about you, Maxie, in my part of town. The whispers are that you know something about some balls." The largest of them came right up to Max's desk.

"Shera Lightbox, aren't you far out from your turf?" Max asked.

"My turf is wherever I say it is," Shera countered. He put his hands on Max's desk and leaned in. "I hear from my lads down at the docks you might know about some old magic thing that can make me a lot of bills."

"Does the Ro mob know you're in Goblin Town? Skullcrusher won't take kindly to you and your goons showing up unannounced," Max told them.

"Maxie, Maxie, Maxie... You seem to put way too much stock in that old goblin's ability to run his territory. Now, whatever you're into, I want it."

"All I'm doing is chasing down leads on a couple of murders," Max stated.

"Murders?" Shera laughed long and hard. When he recovered, he glanced back at his boys. "Meist thinks Maxie here feels he has privilege today. Lads, let him know he doesn't."

Two of the hulking brutes came at Max.

There was a beating, and Max took the brunt. After Max received more than a few kicks while he was down, Shera called off his beasts.

"Now, Max, when you get the thing, I want you to bring it over to my camp. It would be bad for you to give it to Mhi'ro and his boys. Understand?"

Max nodded. "Sure."

"Good! We're all friends again then. Come on, lads. More bills, shells, and stones to gather back at home," Shera said as he and his enforcers left.

Max got to his feet and sat again. He looked down the hall through the open office door. One thing he knew: if a full member of a mob wants you beat, it was best to just take the beating. To fight back could and would get you killed for sure.

He poured a full glass of gaile, drank it down, and then got up and closed his door, which was now a bit wobbly on its hinges. He went over to the basin, looked at his bruised face in the mirror, and touched an inch-long cut over his eyebrow.

After cleaning himself up, he sat down and took another slug from the bottle. He then locked up and headed for his apartment.

Snow was falling again, obscuring visibility. He crossed 52nd Street and turned onto Pewter, a side street with a long line of old three-story bluestones stretching to 53rd. At the corner of Pewter, he turned onto Lipton. The gawdy brass and glass doors of 1758 53rd and Lipton stood before him. Felix was standing there, dressed neatly in his uniform. He had manicured nails and a stern expression on his face. He was a very intimidating ogre indeed.

"How are you today, Mister Draber? You look a bit worse for wear."

"Thanks for asking, Felix. Oh, and you can call me Max."

Felix smiled. "The informality of it, sir. I cannot abide by it. Kind of you to offer, though."

Max nodded. He headed toward the lift, rang for the car, and rode it to the seventh floor. Down at the end of the hall, he came to his door, slipped in his key, and went in.

He tossed his hat onto the rack, followed by his overcoat and jacket. Through the window, he watched the snow plummeting to the street and piling up on the outside sill.

After sitting on the couch, he reached over and turned on the lamp. The walls were covered in fading green-and-gold paper, some of which was peeling at the edges by the ceiling.

He put his feet up on the cocktail table, fished around in the corner of the sofa, and retrieved a bottle of gaile. He pulled the cork and took a long draft.

Those forest-green walls were closing in on him. He could hear the auto-guns spraying their golden death out there...in the woods just beyond the trenches. His feet were frozen in the mud, the cold wind chipping away at them, exposing flesh and bone to its vicious bite. The snipers were out there too. So were the mockers, the officers, and the grenadiers.

Max's eyes were shut tight. He rocked back and forth, trying to block out the sounds. Even covering his ears was useless; the sounds were not coming from outside, but inside his head. Another slug of gaile, then another. He opened his eyes; the sounds stopped. He was in his living room, surrounded by green wallpaper with gold accents.

Getting the bottle back onto the cocktail table was difficult, but he finally made it. It took a few tries for him to get on his feet and make a serpentine stroll to the bed. He collapsed and drifted into darkness.

THE VOCALRELAY WAS buzzing loudly. Max rolled over onto his side and groped for the receiver.

"Ya?" He sat up. "You don't say? I understand." Max looked at his wrist-clock. "I'll be there in an hour." He hung up. A knock at the door echoed loudly. "Just a minute! Keep your shirt on!" Max fetched the pistol from his overcoat and approached the door.

"Who is it?" Max barked.

"William!"

Max unlocked the door and opened it. The dwarf rushed in. "There's a black Paddington following me." He rushed to the window, pulled over a chair, climbed up, and looked out the window. "See...down there." William pointed.

Max pulled William off the chair. "Get away from there. If they knew to follow you, they know where I live and are probably watching the windows." He locked the door again. "What's the rumple? Why the hotfoot coming over here?"

"By the gods! What happened to your face? Did you get hit by a cart?" William stared at Max's head.

"No," Max stated curtly. "Why are you here?"

"A man came to see me. He wanted me to find out about a rumor that someone in the underworld got their hands on the Turin Balls. When I assured him there was no such thing that I was aware of, his flunky kicked me a few times, then threatened to shave off my beard! My beard, Max! How crude."

Max sat on his bed. "Calm down. What did they look like?"

"One of them was refined—an aristocrat, I think. His toady was elf with a burned face and peg leg." William pulled the chair by the bed and climbed up and sat. "This damn thing is definitely not built for my kind," he added.

"Peg leg?" Max was assertive. "You're sure he had a false leg and burns on his face?"

"Absolutely. He was this close to my face with a cutthroat razor!" William earnestly stated while demonstrating the distance with his stubby fingers.

Max dropped the shades and peered out. The private steam car was down there. He looked across at the other buildings; he didn't see anyone obvious looking back. He looked up along the roofline; again, no one appeared to be there.

"Look...this is all getting sticky now," Max said. "You'd better pay for a couple of guards to keep an eye on your place and employees. Whoever that is down there, they're working for someone with sacks of bills."

Max quickly dressed. On went the coat and then the overcoat. He slipped the pistol into the pocket.

"Come on. We'll beat it out the side door. You go back to your shop. I've got some business to attend to." Max motioned for William to come to the door. Max took out the pistol, opened the door, and checked the hallway. All clear. He let William out and locked his door behind himself, and then they both went to the stairwell.

Once in the lobby, Max checked the room. "A shady guy over there and one that looks like a chump by the door. Looks pretty normal. Come on," Max said.

They slipped out and down a side passage. It connected to another hallway, and they came to a door that locked from the inside. Max turned the handle and peeked outside—just an empty alleyway with some snow built up around the sides.

In an instant, the two were outside. Max walked William a block away from the building. He hailed a steam carriage and sent William packing. A moment later, Max was headed down to the 20th Precinct.

He checked several times but didn't see the errant Paddington. Once at the station, Max paid the driver and quickly entered the constable station. It took only a moment for Jonstone to arrive.

"What's got you spooked? Who gave you a beating?" Jonstone asked.

"Spooked? Beating?" Max looked offended. "Come on, Nick. I'm here to find out what you found out down in that underhall?"

Jonstone shook his head. "You're a bad liar, Max. Or...maybe you're a really good one. I'm not sure which way the wind blows on that." He pulled out a smoke, put it in his mouth, and lit it. "Anyway, you were right. Lots of stolen property down in those passages. We also found an old gun there. It was recently fired. Damn thing had a defect in the breach, and it's possible that someone might have gotten burned. You don't have any burns on you, do you, Max?"

Max shook his head. "No burns here. So, was it the weapon that killed Tararill?"

Jonstone took a long drag and blew out an acrid cloud into the room. "It was."

"You're welcome," Max said. "You got some evidence courtesy of your favorite private detective."

"Now, I want to know what you know," Jonstone said.

"Look...there is someone with a pedigree trailing me now. And I was asked to pay a visit to the Updike, Hallion, and Pickersleve insurance company. They said they had an insurance bond out for a missing relic and wanted it found," Max told Jonstone.

"They wanted to hire you?" Jonstone chuckled. "Will wonders never cease? Okay, what's the skinny?"

"I'm not sure yet. I'll have more for you in a couple of days," Max stated. "And if you got someone keeping an eye on me, stop it. I've got plenty followers, and I don't need more!"

Jonstone nodded. "You don't have to worry about that, Max. None of my men are trailing you. In fact, I'm actually wagering that you'll get killed before this is all over. Why would I blow my bet by helping you out?"

Max laughed. "Same old Jonstone. Never in anyone's corner but your own." Max went to the door and looked out through its plate-glass windows. No Paddington. He exited.

"Where you off to, Max?" Jonstone called after him.

"Off to see a working girl's boss," Max replied.

"You have no shame." Jonstone turned and vanished up some stairs.

Max hailed a steam carriage.

A few minutes later, he was strolling along Longreach Street on his way to see Tararill's madam. She wasn't far. In fact, he saw her sitting on the stairs leading up to a tall three-story bluestone.

"Herodite Malincot," Max called out.

Herodite stood. Her long black hair was luminous. Her eyes were white—no pupil to be seen—and her lips blood-red. "As I live and breathe! Max Draber, the shadow that darkens my door. Someone ask you the hard way, Max? You look like you've seen better days."

Max stopped at the bottom of the steps. "I always look like this. How's business?"

"Never a problem here in Goblin Town. I have powerful friends and a license that is without reproach." She smiled, and her teeth radiated a white light that was almost blinding. "Looking for a part-time lover? Or just passing through?"

"Tararill," Max said.

"Poor girl. Terrible business her being murdered. I have something special for whoever did it. If you find out, Max, I'll pay extra to have at them first," Herodite said as her hands faded to black then back to glowing white.

"That's what I'm here about. Her last bobo? Who was he?" Max took out his pipe and lit it.

Herodite seemed to be contemplating something. "I guess it would be folly not to tell you." She made an archaic symbol in the air with her fingers, and a piece of paper appeared in her hand. "If this leads to the murderer, I'll pay handsomely to carve him up into bits over a very long time." She handed the note to Max.

The paper was warm, as if it had just come from atop a burning stove. "Thanks. As things progress, I'll keep your offer in mind."

Herodite smiled again. "As you wander the cold city streets and become weary, come back to see me. I'll take you to my private room. I'll breathe life back into you at a discount, Max."

Max took a few steps as he opened the note and read the name. He froze and turned back. "Is this true?"

"As true as the day waits for night," Herodite stated. "Come again, Max. Next time, I'll love your wretched soul, and you'll never stop thanking me for it!"

Grinning, Max turned and walked down the street. He shouted for a carriage and was off again.

Chapter 6

A Nobel Pursuit

THE STEAM CARRIAGE halted in front of the New Gate Public Works building on 26th Street. A wide stone staircase led to a massive portico held up by six stark white fluted columns. Massive brass doors provided access, and Max took little time to enter.

The stagnant smell of age immediately assaulted Max's nostrils, and old-style gas fixtures, now converted to electric lights, hung low in the rotunda. Various employees rushed about, most dressed in dark suits and wearing toppers or Croquor felt hats. There were others there too: some tradesmen who did work in the tunnels and sewers and the occasional dutiful patron searching for the correct office to pay a bill or buy a license to serve liquor and/or lust.

Max went to the information desk. "I'm looking for Mister Highloe Barrington's office."

The young human female chuckled. "Mister Barrington? The director of Public Works? No one even gets close to his office without an appointment. I suggest you call next time and make one." She turned to another person, who stepped up to the desk.

Laying his hand on her arm, Max directed her back to him. "Sister, how and who?"

She looked annoyed now. "Unhand me, you flibert! I should call security... What happened to your face? Are you sure you don't want a constable?" She looked deep into Max's eyes and caught her breath. She brushed off the other person and leaned in a bit toward Max. "So, you're not half bad a looker for a masher with a busted lip. What's your name, flibert?"

"Max Draber."

"Well, Max, if you're interested in how to set up a visit with Mister Barrington, I get off work in an hour, and you can buy me a snort. Maybe even lunch?"

Max stood up as tall as he could. A grin formed across his face. "Sure. Meet me at Dolly's just down the street."

"Mmm... Can't wait."

Max turned to go but stopped and turned back. He examined her name tag. "Wroandra," he said aloud, looking into her eyes again.

"See you in an hour, Max Draber."

MAX WAS ON HIS SECOND gaile when Wroandra entered. She looked around the room, found Max, and headed to his table.

"I see you have an unfair advantage over me." She nodded toward the empty glass in front of Max.

"Unfair?" Max waved the waiter over. "Another for me, and the lady will have a pink hooter."

Wroandra chuckled. "How did you know I liked pink hooters?"

Max shrugged with a whimsical smile. "Lucky guess." He sat back. "How long have you been employed with the Public Works Department?"

"Three years. I started cleaning toilets and was promoted to information attendant," Wroandra stated. "How about you? What do you do that allows you to talk with the big hodok at Public Works? Sales? Engineer?"

"Snoop, actually," Max said.

"What does that mean?"

Max took out his pipe and sparked it up. "A shoe-leather peeper, a private dick, a personal detective."

"Really? Like in the Nole Vesper books?" Wroandra asked excited. "I ain't never met a real one before. What's it like?"

Max played up the business. After all, it wasn't really very exciting most of the time. He lavished her with some stories of roughs and mobsters and then shifted his talk to informants.

The waiter brought the drinks and took their lunch order. A short while later, after a few drinks had been consumed, the food arrived. It took little time to devour the cuisine.

Max sat back. "So, you said something about teaching me how to get an appointment with the boss."

"It's not easy," Wroandra said. "He's awful busy. Every time I see him walk by, he's coming from or going to a meeting with someone rich or noble." She took up her drink and sipped it. "I know his secretary well. I can get you on his manifest. When do you want to see him?"

"How's tomorrow after the midmorning break?" Max suggested.

"I'll see what I can do. Shall I give you a blast on the blower? Or how about I come visit you tonight and let you know in person that you're on the list?"

Max took out his pen and scrawled his address on a napkin. "Come on up. Ring the bell twice, wait a second, then twice again. I'll know it's you."

Wroandra's excitement was apparent. Max was counting on her love of intrigue and detective books to play up the silly buzzer ploy. She was all in.

After paying the bill, Max walked her out. She headed up the street, and he hailed a carriage. A moment later, he was back at his office. There was a notegram stuck in his doorjamb.

He sat in his office chair and opened the envelope. It was from Limiric.

To Max Draber,

> *Stranger lurking around the beach house. Looks like a grimalden—yellow skin, pointy tail, horns. Come as soon as you can. I'm scared.*

Max picked up the vocalrelay, dialed the number, and waited. Limiric picked up on the second ring.

"Hey, sugar doll. It's me. Is the grimalden still skulking about?" Max asked.

"He left a few hours ago. Where have you been? I'm scared, Max—real scared!"

"How did you figure out someone was lurking there?"

"There are lights that show when someone is near the house. I looked through one of the scopes and I saw him," Limiric said.

"Ah – well don't give it a second thought. The mug is a guy working for an insurance dealer here in town. He's looking for an insured relic I suspect your husband had." Max fished out a glass and pulled out the gaile bottle. "Have you ever heard of an antique called the Turin Balls?"

"Turin Balls?" Limiric sounded confused. "What in the name of the dark ones is that?"

"An antique... Maybe a relic. Tell me... Did your husband ever show you a special purchase he might have made?"

"Once, shortly before he died, he brought me to the National One High Gate Bank on 30th Street. He gave me an envelope to put in our strongbox. I did so without question," Limiric told Max.

"Did you look inside the envelope?"

"No, but it felt like a key," Limiric stated.

"Okay, stay there. I'll be by in a couple of days. I need to check a few more things out here...make sure it's safe for you to come back. Then I'll come for you."

"Okay. Please hurry."

"You're safe there for now. Sit tight. I'll see you soon." Max hung up the receiver.

He finished his drink and put the bottle back in the drawer. It took a few hours of paperwork for Max to finish his day. Outside the sky was darkening, and the snow began to fall again.

He put on his overcoat, locked up, and headed out to the street. Just across the way, Tararill had lain. *Had she been coming to see me? Or...?*

Max hailed a carriage and headed home. "1758 53rd and Lipton."

"Really, Max? That's only a few stones for me," the carriage driver stated disappointed.

"Sorry, Danboy. I'll make it a fiver for your trouble." Max pulled out a crumpled five royal bill and dropped it over the front seat.

"All right! Thanks Max." Danboy looked at Max in his review mirror. "Ya look dragged out. Someone thump ya a little? Don't worry. I'll drop you."

"Thanks. And I don't want to talk about it." Max suddenly felt the weight of the investigation squarely about his shoulders.

The steam carriage rattled forward and down the street. The driver made the second right and drove on for two blocks. Danboy rumbled to a halt, releasing some steam from the overpressure valve causing a burst of white mist just outside the right-side passenger door.

Max waited a minute then opened the portal and stepped out onto the sidewalk. "See ya around, Danboy. Don't take any golden stones."

Danboy chuckled. "No worthless stones for me." He hefted a truncheon and slapped it into the palm of his hand a few times. "Them mugs know better than to try and dump funny money on this cabbie."

Max smiled and nodded. He turned and walked into his apartment building. Felix, the door ogre, let Max pass.

"Good evening, Mister Draber," Felix stated.

"Felix, I've told you many times. You can call me Max."

"Very good, Mister Draber. I'll keep that in mind," Felix told Max as he passed. "Oh. The elevator is out, sir."

Max stopped, exhaled loudly through his nose, and then headed for the stairwell. Up the wooden steps he went. It felt like he was climbing Mount Skyfather with each labored step, floor after floor.

He fished out his key, opened the door, and entered the darkened room. He walked over to the standing lamp and rotated the switch. A cascade of soft light invaded the space. The lampshade's red, blue, and green crystals bathed the couch and chair in a fairy-like glow.

He'd just finished his first glass of gaile when there was a knock at the door. He went over and peeped out the spy hole. Wroandra stood there dressed in a long, gray woolen coat and a red-brim hat with a feather sticking out of the top.

"Well, maybe not such a rotten day after all," Max whispered.

He opened the door, and she came in.

"I got you on the meeting roster for ten fifteen tomorrow morn," she said.

"Fantastic! Drink?" Max asked.

"Wine or a yates with soda."

Max went to the wet bar and brought the drink back over to her. "You're a resourceful lady."

"I have my talents," she said coyly.

"I owe you a fine dinner after we finish these drinks. I hope you like giant cuisine. I know a little restaurant downtown called Vandenburg's."

"Vandenburg's?" Wroandra repeated excitedly. "Can you get a reservation on such short notice?"

"You don't worry about that, sugar. I know a few people," Max replied.

"Well, I'll be sure to dress for that occasion like I did for this one." She dropped her overcoat and exposed her naked body.

Max was taken aback. A grin spread across his face. The long day faded, and his second wind gathered in his sails. He looked at her with lustful desire.

He took her by the hand and led her into the bedroom. "You did bring something other than your coat to wear, didn't you?"

Wroandra giggled. "I'm not a donker, Max. I thought ahead. Got all I need right in my purse. But my dress doesn't cover much."

"Can't wait to see it," Max stated as he fell onto his bed pulling Wroandra with him.

MAX AND WROANDRA STOOD outside the back door of Vandenburg's. The latch clicked, and the portal opened. A grumpy-looking troll in a tall chef's hat stood there.

"Max? Did you lose a fight or something?" the cook asked. "Who's the snack?"

"Gingma," Max replied, "This is my lady friend, and let's not complicate things with names. How's the sauté business?"

"Profitable and exciting. How's the snoop business?"

"Scary and violent," Max replied.

Gingma smirked. "That explains the face. Same as always then."

Max chuckled. "So? Can we come in?"

"Ah, yes. Come in. Bing is the table manager for the night." Gingma stepped aside and let Max and Wroandra enter.

Max took Wroandra by the hand and led her through the kitchen, down a hallway, and into the main dining room of the restaurant. He flagged down a waiter, who then went and got the table manager.

The dark-haired elf stood a head taller than Max. He had a long face, pointy nose, and stern green eyes that looked down upon Max and Wroandra.

Bing's eyes widened for a moment as he viewed Max's wounds. "Well, as I live and breathe! If it ain't Max Draber. What's the haps, Max?"

"Bing," Max said with a nod, "can you fit us in somewhere?"

Bing surveyed the room. He looked at the waiter. "Set up a table over there by the stage—space nineteen. Also, bring a bottle of blue Url Ma Drire over." Bing looked at Max. "Covered by the establishment. You know—for that thing you did for us." He looked back at the waiter. "Take their coats to the checker, and bring them the ticket."

"Thanks, Bing. You haven't seen Shera, have you?" Max asked.

"Not all night. Do you want me to let him know you're here?"

"No," Max said quickly. "I mean, I know how to reach him if I need to."

Bing's expression didn't change. "Then I'll keep you out of my conversation with him if he shows."

Max slipped the elf a twenty. "Thanks, Bing. You're one of the good ones."

"For a friend, that would be accurate to say," Bing replied.

The waiter showed Max to the table. The corner was dimly lit, and on the square table sat a candle burning inside a yellow stained glass container.

"May I bring you some specialty drinks?" the waiter asked.

Max tucked a fiver into the server's shirt pocket. "The lady will have a yates and soda, and I'll have a Whipet—no ice."

The waiter vanished into the crowd.

"What did you do for the restaurant that they're giving all this free stuff?" Wroandra asked.

"Nothing much. A little issue with a hoodlum and some protection money. Nothing big. Tell me about Mister Barrington?" Max asked.

"He has a noble title. I think it's Warrior of the Front, Second King Protector."

"Really? Did he fight in the war?" Max asked.

Wroandra laughed. "Of course not. I believe he paid for a company of locals to go in his place. During the war, I asked one of the office whelps why he wasn't going to fight. He told me that Mister Barrington once became visibly shaken at the suggestion."

The drinks arrived along with a bottle of blue Url Ma Drire. After taking their order, the server dashed off into the throng again.

"So, he stayed in the city?" Max asked.

"He was here in the department the whole time. I did hear that he consolidated his power by arranging for some of the other board members authorities to be folded into his position. You know, like accounts payable and shipping. It is rumored that he is quite corrupt." Wroandra took a drink of her yates, sat back in her dark purple-and-gold gossamer dress, and crossed her bare legs. "You never said what you wanted the boss for."

Max drank down half of his gaile. "I have a few questions for him regarding a case I'm working."

"What case?"

"I'm not at liberty to say yet. But seeing how you helped me out, I can tell you it might be a bestseller if churned into a tawdry novel."

Wroandra leaned forward and put her elbows on the table. She traced a strange pattern on the table with her finger as she smiled. "I got all night, Mister Snoop. And I hear you stalker-peepers can go the distance when it comes to all-nighters."

Max swallowed hard. "It would be rude of me to contradict you on our first dinner, so let's get a couple more drinks and finish this bottle of blue Url Ma Drire. Then, you can describe to me what you had in mind."

A grin grew across Wroandra's face, reminding Max of an adolescent dragon toying with its prey. Max flagged down the waiter and got more drinks. Shortly after, their dinners arrived, and they feasted like it was year-end.

"Maxie, Maxie, Maxie," said a voice over Max's shoulder.

He turned in his chair and saw Shera standing there in an evening formal. The mobster's two goons were not far off.

"Evening, Shera," Max said.

"What happened to your face? Fall down some stairs or something?"

"Something like that," Max said.

"Did you get my thing yet?" Shera asked.

"Not yet. Getting close. No need to worry. You'll get what's owed you."

"Glad to hear it." Shera took Wroandra by the hand and kissed it. "Such a lovely flower." Wroandra giggled. "Make sure you get it soon, Maxie boy. My patience is being tested, and I don't like tests." He nodded to his henchmen, and they all maneuvered through the crowd across the room to a booth.

Max exhaled loudly.

"Are you okay?" Wroandra asked.

"Yes, of course. Just surprised. Didn't expect to see him here tonight," Max stated. "Let's get out of here."

AS THE CLOCK TRIPPED over to the new day, Max lay in bed. Wroandra was panting and wiping the glistening sweat from her brow.

"What was that called?" she asked.

"It's called the Fatum Donnybrook," Max said. "I read about it in the *Kingdom Kartush Book of a Thousand Pleasures*."

"A thousand pleasures, eh?" Wroandra asked.

Max sat up, lit his pipe, and smoked in the dark for a while. When he was done, he closed the bedroom window and put his pipe in the holder. "Let's get some sleep. I need to be fresh for the morning."

Wroandra snuggled up against Max. It was cold in the room, even though the radiator was doing its best to warm the place.

It took only a few minutes for Wroandra to drift off. Max struggled, his mind fighting against his desperate need for sleep. The war, the case, Limiric...they all wanted equal time with his loud inner monologue—and they all got what they wanted.

Max rolled over and found his companion gone. She'd left early—sometime while he'd been in an exhaustive black sleep. The air was frosty, biting at his exposed flesh with icicle fangs. He slipped out of the sheets and into his robe and slippers. From there, he made it to the washroom and tidied up.

Once he had dressed, he made his way downstairs and to the local diner. Several cups of skull rush later, he was ready to meet Mister Highloe Berrington.

Chapter 7

A Lack of Empathy

THE CITY MANAGEMENT District was bustling. Max pushed his way through the crowd. Dour-faced bureaucrats, shoulder to shoulder, coming and going, with jaws set and eyes staring down at their shoes, moved past him.

He entered the New Gate Public Works building. After passing the information desk, he went up the curved marble staircase to the second floor.

A bell rang, and the lift doors opened. Max stepped in and pressed the button for the fifth floor. A strong smell of age, like that of a library, hung in the air. The door opened with another ding, and Max's eyes fell upon a wide office space with a receptionist sitting at a counter.

"Can I help you?" asked the muscular male elf, who was wearing black garters and a cobalt-colored visor.

"Max Draber to see Mister Berrington."

The elf thumbed through some papers. "Ah. Here you are." He looked at the clock on the wall. "A bit early, but not a problem. Please have a seat in the lounge, and I'll have one of the foundlings bring you a cup of fresh ground hythana."

"That would be great," Max replied.

The receptionist pressed a button, and a young dwarf whose beard only came down to the bottom of his neck came running.

"Sir? How can I improve my station, sir?"

The receptionist stood and handed the foundling a paper card. "Please go to the lounge and provide Mr. Draber a hot fresh cup of hythana. Hurry so he can make his appointment."

"Yes, sir!" the foundling said with all the excitement an apprentice in training can muster.

Max waited patiently for the cup of skull rush. It was not long in coming.

The dwarf packed off, and Max sat sipping his drink. He watched the clock on the wall for some time, and then just as he was ready to walk out, a fairy trailing orange iridescent dust flew in and asked him to follow her. He did.

Max passed by the desks of workers feverishly shuffling papers, scribing, and filing. At the end of the room, they passed through a set of tall brass-strapped double doors. Inside was a room with a fireplace and several clerks. Beyond was another set of doors and Highloe Berrington's office.

"Mr. Draber to see you sir," the fairy stated. She turned around and exited, closing the door behind her.

Without turning around, Berrington blew out a stream of gray smoke into the room.

"Max Draber," he said. "You are a recent addition to my long list of meetings today. Why do you need to see me?" He turned around and walked over to his desk.

Berrington had a round face and bald head. His eyes were close-set, and his nose was broad and a bit upturned. His stocky body was neither fat nor muscular, but his demeanor was authoritative.

Max walked over and handed the man his card. "I'm so glad you could see me today. I'm working for the family of Tararill Tre'hu."

"Who? I'm not familiar with the name," Berrington countered.

"Ah. I'm sorry. I was under the impression she worked for you."

Berrington stiffened a bit. "I have never had anyone by that name in my employ."

Max sat in one of the fluffy leather-bound chairs in front of Berrington's desk. "I see. I must be misinformed. My apologies," Max retorted. "But perhaps you could give it a think. She wasn't exactly on your payroll here at the office...or a domestic at your ample home under the direction of your wife..."

"How dare you!" Berrington blurted.

Max smiled. "I often dare, Mister Berrington. It's part of my business. And any answer you provide to me is only for my investigation. I don't need to involve the constables if I think you are being honest with me."

Berrington's face went beet red. His fists clenched, and he moved over to his chair and picked up his vocalrelay receiver.

"Police or private goons?" Max asked. "I don't mind the bronzies, but I would care of it if you tried to rough-handle me. Put down the blower, and just answer my questions." Max took out his pipe and lit a match.

Staring into Max's eyes, Berrington leered and then slowly put the receiver down. He sat. "What questions?"

"See? Much better to be civil than rude, don't you think?" Max took out his small flip pad and a pencil. "When did you start seeing Tararill?"

Berrington thought on this for some time. "A few years back. She was sent to my city loft on 22nd as a gift by a...campaign contributor."

"Above the law or under it?" Max asked, the question delineating whether the patron was a noble or criminal.

"A friend." Berrington took a puff from his cigar. "Now, kindly leave my office."

"Not quite yet." Max stood up. "She was murdered just a few days ago. Landed in my lap, so to speak. Who sent her as a gift to you?" Max's voice betrayed no nonsense.

Berrington sat in his high-backed brown leather chair. "Look...if I tell you, they'll kill me."

"Who will kill you, sir?" Max pressed.

"You know. Down in...Goblin Town," Berrington whispered.

"Why?"

"The female. She knew something about a device that could be useful to the city." Berrington appeared to be rallying.

"What device?"

"Some sort of archaic antique. They claimed it can turn water into steam using magic. I really don't know much more than that."

The door to the office opened, and Max spun around. A tall, muscular elf limped in and stood there, a great brooding frown across his scarred face. His left eye was missing, and an odd hexagonal-shaped golden earring hung from his right earlobe. Max gave serious scrutiny to the elf's face and could plainly see the white marks of some recent peroxide burns.

"Pip!" Berrington blurted. "Thank the gods you're here! Show this man out."

"You? Time for you to leave," Pip told Max. "I don't know how you got on the director's list of meetings for today, but your time is up."

"A big nasty piece of work you are," Max said to Pip. "I'm going. But one more question, Mister Berrington. Why murder the girl? What value was in it?"

Berrington was silent. He motioned for Pip to take over. The powerful elf limped toward Max at an accelerated pace. His hands reached for Max's coat but found only air.

"Easy, shaky golem!" Max said as he kicked out at the attacker's shin and spun around the outstretched arms. But instead of a solid strike to the elf's leg, there was a hollow-sounding thump.

Pip turned and came at Max again. "That'll cost ya, you pixy prick!"

"Leg gone missing, mate?" Max headed for the door just ahead of Pip.

As Max exited, he ran into two other security men who held him fast. Pip approached.

"Throw him out so he knows not to come back," Pip told them.

The security men nodded and gave Max a hurried beating—punches to the kidneys and stomach—and then promptly dragged him downstairs and threw him out the front door onto the cement walkway. Max rolled once and landed with his arm and hand in the gutter.

Pip showed up in the doorway. "Draber, if you're smart, you'll stick to following cheaters and chasing down insurance frauds. Don't come back here." Pip tossed Max's hat onto the walkway.

Max clambered to his feet and brushed off the dirty snow from his coat and pants. "You'd better get those P burns looked at soon, or you might lose that other eye."

Pip scowled and touched the injuries with his left hand. "Don't come back." He turned and went back into the building.

Max walked to the end of the block, waved down a carriage, and set off to see Jonstone.

"Now, what is it?" Jonstone asked, his appearance a bit disheveled.

"The ox face you picked up from the hotel...did he spill anything?" Max asked.

Jonstone walked around Max and then stopped directly in front of the man. "Do you moonlight as a gym's punching sack? Every time I see you of late, you're sporting more bruises and cuts than a fisticuff flinger."

"Did he tell you anything?" Max persisted.

"The mug refused to talk, but we found in his flat a bundle of cash hidden under his bed with a note and a description of a female goblin. He was up to his neck in no good." Jonstone pulled out a smoke and fired it up.

"What type of paper?" Max asked.

"Paper?" Jonstone was confused.

"Ya. Was it the expensive, thick, bonded kind you'd find downtown at a proctor's place or attorney's office?"

"Come on. I know you'll hang about my neck like a golden torc if you don't see it for yourself." Jonstone led the way, and Max followed.

A moment later, they were in Jonstone's office. The elf went to a cabinet and removed a folder. He put it on the desk. "Take a look. You tell me what you think."

Max took the note in hand and felt it with his fingers. "Heavy," he said. He held it up to the light and then chuckled. "They thought they were so clever." He handed it to Jonstone. "See for yourself."

When the paper was held up, it was clear there was a watermark. It was hard to read, but when held just right to the light, it spelled the letters N.G.P&S. "What does it mean?"

"It means the murderer killed Tararill on the order of someone working at the New Gate Power and Steam building."

"Who?" Jonstone asked.

"When I find out, you'll find out." Max headed for the door.

"Where are you going?" Jonstone looked annoyed.

"To find out!" Max said and made for the exit.

Max stopped by William's antique shop. He was met at the desk by the dwarf.

"Max, what brings you back here?" William asked.

"The Turin Balls. Any word amongst the relic traders?"

William shrugged. "Not much. Evidently, a month back, someone wanted an appraiser to come look at some possible magic item. Later, a few of the more unsavory traders met to discuss the item. One of them was connected to the Mhi'ro mob."

"Mhi'ro?" Max said. "Okay, that complicates things."

"They said it was used to heat a small traveling boiler. They made some electricity for the crowd, then shuffled it off before anyone could get a closer look at it. Smells like dragon dung, if you ask me. That's all I got. Sorry it isn't more, Max." William put two glasses on the counter and decanted some liquor into them. "Have a snort."

Max shot back the brew and then headed for the door. "Thanks, mate!" he called over his shoulder as he sailed through the door.

"Watch out for the Mhi'ro mob! They'll cut up your pretty face," William shouted after Max.

Max arrived at the docks. He wove his way through the steam-powered lifters and cranes and found his feet at a two-story warehouse. The side door was open, and he went inside.

"Hey, have you seen Brittle Bart?" Max asked the first longshore worker he came to.

"Aye. The bloke is over by receiving today," the brawny fellow said.

"Thanks!" Max headed across the imposing structure. Once on the other side, he looked about for a large elf with a clipboard. It didn't take long to find him.

"Well, as I live and drink! Max Draber!" Bart called out.

"How's the skirts and shirts, Brittle?" Max replied.

"Like sticking your wilson into a pixie nest!"

Both men laughed at this.

"You look troubled. What's the shaking?" Bart asked.

"Simple question, but don't bother telling me if it'll get you killed. When did Shera find out about the Turin Balls?"

Bart looked surprised. "Turin Balls?"

"Ya. A box that heats water for boilers."

"How the hell did you know about that?" Bart asked.

"He came and told me to keep an eye out for it. So, when did he find out?" Max persisted.

"Few days ago. Some chump done spilled it when the Lightboxers did a collection of some back rent. He said he done seen the thing working in a tunnel up in Goblin Town." Bart leaned up against a wall and lit up a smoke. "He knows it's worth a bundle of bills. You looking for it for Shera?"

"Ya. He asked me," Max lied. "Who was the chump?"

"Micky the Fitter, over off 42nd Avenue. He's one of those dwarf-and-a-halfs." Bart made a disgusted face. "You can find him in the medical ward. I think he's healing up from a busted set of fingers."

"Ward of Mercy? Or Basilica of Hearts?" Max asked.

"Mercy...I think."

"Thanks, pal!" Max stuffed a fiver into Bart's shirt pocket. "See ya round."

The trip back up town took a few minutes. Max got out of the carriage in front of the Ward of Mercy medical hall. Inside, he quickly made for the room that Micky was in, and went directly there.

"What's the rumble, Micky?" Max asked.

Sitting up, Micky looked surprised. "Max Draber?"

"The one and only."

"You still toting a bronze shield?" Micky asked.

"Naw. Traded it in to work as a private detective." Max pulled out his pipe. "I heard you ran into some elf troubles?"

"No. I...got my fingers caught in a doorjamb. That's all. Could happen to anyone," Micky replied.

"Well, you told them something about a magic box and some floating balls. All I want to know is what it looked like."

Micky thought on this. "What's in it for me?"

"A few bills and me not telling Shera that you been talking to the constables."

Micky grew nervous. "Look...I just paid that nutter off, and ain't going to bet on them games of chance no more. I ain't never chummed up to bronzies, and I ain't going to now."

"Look...Shera's not going to take that risk. You and I both know it. Just tell me what I want to know. You can make a pile of roy bills, and I can get my information." Max blew some smoke into the room.

Micky looked around. "Okay. Here's what I seen. A fellow done brought out a contraption like a cabinet. He connected a hose to a small boiler tied to a generator. He fiddled with some knobs and switches, then opened a panel on the face of the thing. It had three floating balls that were slowly spinning. They spun faster and faster. Suddenly, the boiler was steaming, and the gen was generating. He turned on a wireless, and we all listened to some music. Then he shut it all down and whisked the cabinet off down a tunnel. A fella told us it was for sale and that because it was a magic item, it was expensive. I tell ya, Max, it was magic, if ever I've seen it."

"Who else was there?" Max asked.

"Some fancy types. Jinx the Fumbler was there, as was Tory the Stonybock. Also, there was this fell'er in a long coat with a limp. Nasty-looking elf with a scar on his face."

Max took a drag from his pipe and exhaled. "Who was showing the thing?"

"Some goblin. I ain't never seen him before. Gray scales about his eyes, black nails, and blinked a lot."

"Where was this?" Max pressed.

"In the down-under. You know, the steam pipes and cables and such. Not far from the Longview Bakery," Micky stated.

"How much was he asking?"

"Six million Royal Bills," Micky said. "Way out of my league."

Max sat on the edge of the bed and whistled a single note. "Six million?" Max asked surprised. "Damn pricey. Not many could afford it. What were you doing there?"

"Ya. No short order for sure," Micky said. "I was a proxy for a buyer. Some red-bearded dapper with an accent. From the mainland, I think. A Westerner."

Max stood up and tossed a ten-bill note on the bed. "Thanks, Micky. This is between you and I now. Don't worry about Shera." He slipped out the door and back onto the snowy street.

Chapter 8

A Dicey Trip

MAX CAUGHT A STEAM carriage uptown. The driver dropped him off at the Sutro Capital Station. He caught a coach across the river into Surgy Town and then another down the coast to Limpet.

"Where ya heading, lopper?" asked the steam carriage driver.

"12547 Lindsey Passway, Sinclair Beach," Max said.

The driver engaged the wheels, and the vehicle churned out along the street and toward the resort homes.

It took twenty minutes to reach, and soon Max saw the three- and four-story estate homes that extended south along the shoreline. The carriage slowed and stopped.

Max paid the driver and asked him to stay. Straight away, he headed into the home via the seaside-overlook glass door. Once inside, he moved to the secured suite and used the vocalrelay to let Limiric know he was there.

"I'm so glad you've come!" Limiric said.

"Grab your stuff. We're heading back," Max told her.

She showed up at the door with her travel case. "Okay. What's happened? Am I safe?"

Max reached over and took her bag. "Come on. Daylight is burning. We need to have a look in that strongbox you have."

An hour later, Max and Limiric pulled up in front of the National One High Gate Bank. Once they were inside, Max accompanied Limiric into the private viewing booth with the box.

She opened it, and inside was a variety of things. She pulled out a gray envelope, opened it, and poured out an old-fashioned key onto the table.

"What an odd-looking key!" Limiric said.

Max picked it up and examined it. "I know someone who might help."

They left the bank and traveled to William's antique shop.

"Hi, Max. What's shaking?" William asked.

"Got a minute, Bill?" Max asked.

"Sure. Come into my office." William led the way to his personal space. He sat behind his desk and took out three glasses. "Some New Brighton Port?"

"Sure," Max said. "Have a look at this." He plunked the key onto William's desk.

"Ge-gob and licorice tarts!" William blurted out. "It's a magic hallman key." He shot back his port and picked up the device. "I've seen only one in my life, and I think there are only five that are known to exist."

"Worth a bill or two?" Max asked.

"There are those in the dark markets that would pay a hundred thousand bills just to touch it." William poured himself another drink. "Where in the name of the hokey-mac did you get this?"

"It belonged to my husband," Limiric stated.

"Look, Bill. Did these types of keys open cabinets?" Max was direct.

William continued to look at the key as if expecting someone to shout, "Got ya!"

"Bill!" Max said more loudly.

"Yes... It could be used for that." William poured himself another and then sipped his drink as he put the key down and looked up at Max. "What are you suggesting?"

"There was that showing of a magic item in the underways sometime back. Someone was providing a viewing of a magic steam-making machine. They used it to power a generator and make electricity and run a wireless. Ring any bells?" Max wore his no-nonsense face.

"Sounds like what I told you. But I swear I was not made aware, nor did I attend such a thing!" The hurt at having been left out was apparent in William's eyes. "How dare they keep me out of that!" He slammed his small hand upon the table with a thud.

"Who?" Max asked.

William looked up, startled. "Who? I can't tell you that."

"Bill, I like you. You've been a good friend to me over the years. I say this with all the care and admiration I can muster. If you don't tell me, I'll drop you out a ten-story window."

William cracked a smile. "All that way just to toss me out? Max, you do love me." He took his drink, sat back, and produced a pipe. "You can't tell anyone I've told you."

Max nodded. "I swear I will never tell anyone."

"Okay. Galvant Micknick from Downtown Odd Things; Chin Vin, who owns All Things Old; Donovan G., who runs Magic Items Inc.; and Piper Tallman, who owns The Leaping Horse. When you include me, we make up the cabal controlling the trade of magic items in the city. It's not a lot, nor has it ever been much of a dangerous business. Mostly oddities and silly nonsense collectors crave."

"So, they cut you out for some reason?" Max mused.

"It would seem." William put down his drink, lit a match, and puffed on his pipe, blowing dark smoke into the room.

"Why?" Max asked.

William looked at Max. "They never really liked me, you know. After the war, I had a few ships' worth of old-world magic items that I liberated from the Bangle Continent. They only let me into the syndicate because I had so much stored away. If they offended me, they knew I could flood the market, and they'd all go under. I do know that Piper Tallman has wanted me gone for years."

"If I see him, I'll give him a bash in the chops for you," Max said.

William chuckled. "Thanks. If you find what that key fits, let me know right away. I can be of more help if you have something physical to show me."

Max turned to Limiric. "Can you think of anyplace your husband might hide a cabinet"—Max held his hand up about to his neck—"about so high?"

"We have a basement and an attic in our house," Limiric said.

"Too obvious. But we'll check. Did he have someplace outside the home?" Max asked.

"My husband has a boat down at the marina. It's in dry dock. A medium-sized sailing yacht something like that cabinet could be there." Limiric produced a smoke and lit it. "He was always cagey about that boat."

William shrugged and finished his drink. "If you find anything, ring me up."

Max and Limiric left and caught a steam carriage. It took fifteen minutes to get to the public marina. They found the boat propped up in a dry dock. The port-side ladder hung from the gunwale just far enough to be almost halfway to the keel.

Max boosted Limiric. Her strong legs brushed up against his chest, and he felt the flutter of passion. She grabbed onto the ladder and pulled herself up until she got a foot on one of the rungs.

He took a few steps back, dashed forward, and flung himself upward. His fingers latched onto the bottom rung, and he climbed upward hand over hand. He flopped over the railing, landed on the deck, and caught his breath.

"A bit out of shape?" Limiric asked.

Max shook his head. "Not a bit out of shape. All the way out of shape." He smiled at her. She smirked coyly and looked away.

"Come on. If it's anywhere, it will be down in the main cabin." Limiric led the way.

"Wicky-wicky, ticky-tocky, the magic boxy you'll pass to me promptly," a familiar voice called from the ground. "I suppose you're getting me my magic box?"

Max stopped, turned, and went to the railing. Down over the side were Shera Lightbox and a handful of his cronies, each holding a pipe or knife.

"When did you become a poet?" Max asked.

"Smart-ass!" Shera said. "Come on, Max. You didn't think I'd leave you to find a precious relic worth millions without some supervision? Just pluck it out, and drop it over the side to us. We'll take it from here."

Max swallowed his pride and nodded. "Okay. But what if it's not down there?"

"Then you and your little tricky-tasty will pay a small price for wasting my time," Shera told Max.

Max looked over at Limiric and then turned back to Shera. "Leave the lady out of this. No need to hurt her. I'm the lummox you need to teach a lesson to." Max tried to put the thought of a beating out of his imagination.

"Max, you know me. I'm an equal opportunity bruiser. Human, elf, goblin, dwarf, male, female...if you're in my crosshairs, I'm going to teach a lesson to ya," Shera said then chuckled and waved his hand dismissively. "Now fetch."

Max took Limiric by the hand. "I'll get you away. When you're clear, don't stop running until you get to a constable station."

"What about you?" Limiric's face expressed despair and concern.

"Not the first beating I've taken. Come on. Let's hope there is something down there that we can use to get out of this."

Max opened the wooden pocket doors and descended into the darkness of the upper cabin.

He lit his lighter and, in the dim, flickering yellow glow, looked around. "Nothing here." He pressed on into the back, where the bedroom was. Limiric was close behind.

"This is not part of the boat," Limiric said, running her hand over a finely made wooden cabinet. "I've never seen this thing before today."

Max removed the key from his pocket and inserted it into the box. The front panel illuminated bright purple, and then there was buzzing. He turned the key, opened the top door, and stared at three floating balls of glowing light moving in a circle.

"I didn't believe it," Max said in a whisper. "Amazing..."

"Come on, Max! You're pushing your luck!" shouted Shera. "Bring me my thingy."

Max locked the window and pocketed the key. "Help me carry this thing onto the deck." He grabbed onto one side.

The wooden container was heavy, but they lugged it up the stairs onto the main deck. Once they were on top, Max found a long section of rope and removed his pocketknife. He cut the rope in half and secured one end to the starboard side of the gunwale and handed the other end to Limiric.

"When I lower this thing, you drop over the opposite side and make for the hills. I'll stall them as long as I can," Max said.

Limiric nodded. She moved toward the other side of the boat, gripped the rope tightly, and waited.

"I got to tie it off. Just a second!" Max shouted as he secured the other length of rope around the chest of drawers, looped it through a pully, and tied a hitch around the mast. "Here it comes."

With all his strength, he heaved it up and over the railing. The rope pulled tight as it took the full weight of the thing. Below, Shera's men moved back in fear.

"What are ya doing?" shouted Shera as he lashed out at his scared men. "You mugs get under that! It's worth more than your wretched lives anyway!"

The orcs moved back to receive the item being lowered.

Max nodded to Limiric, and she scampered over the edge and off the boat. He gave her a few seconds to lower herself to the ground, then looked over the edge. "You ready down there?" Max shouted.

"Demons and the underworld, Max!" called back Shera. "Yes! Ready down here! Lower the damned thing!"

Max smiled, went to the hitch, pulled the rope free, and then let it go.

Below, there was a crash. A set of muffled groans echoed up. Max heard crushing wood and metal, followed by curses and threats. In that instant, Max rushed to the other side, grabbed the rope, and leapt over.

He swung down and hit the ground running. Behind, he heard the angry yelling of a mob thirsty for his blood.

Max caught a stilt train and rode it all the way to Main Station. He caught a carriage to a flop he knew was empty; it was across from the park. He was back in Goblin Town and figured that Shera would not start a war just to get him. He picked up the vocalrelay and called up Chi'ra.

"Ya, it's Max. I need a sit-down with the chief. Any chance...? Ah, I see... Not even if I have information regarding the Turin Balls?" There was a pause on the other end. "Okay, I'll be there." He looked at his wrist-clock. "Twenty minutes." Max put down the receiver and peeked out the shaded window. No sign of anyone lurking. He picked up the receiver again and dialed Jonstone.

"Did Mrs. Tre'hu show up there? Okay. Put her on," Max said.

"Hey, sugar! It's me. I got clear. I see you did too. Glad of it. Ya... Okay. You'll be alright for now. Stay there. I'm going to meet someone I hope can fix things for us. Stay put. I'll call in an hour."

Max sat on the orange-and-gold chair facing the door. He put his pistol on his leg. Every minute, he found himself checking his timepiece. At the ten-minute mark, he slipped out and down the street.

Max kept to the shadows and moved from alley to doorway and through shops whose keepers he knew wouldn't ask any questions nor mind him using their back doors. Finally, he entered the diner, where he was met by two muscular goblins with serious expressions.

"Your piece, Draber?" asked one whose scales glistened in the light like a rainbow.

Max surrendered his sidearm, and the other goblin escorted him toward a back booth. There, sipping a cup of tree spice, sat Mhi'ro.

"Max, you seem troubled. Something bothering you? Or should I ask, is someone bothering you?" Mhi'ro smiled.

Max grinned. "You sure know everything in this town."

Mhi'ro sat back. "You wanted to see me about the Turin Balls? Why?"

"I am sure it has something to do with Tararill's death." Max clasped his fingers and set his hands on the table.

"What do you know about it?" Mhi'ro asked.

Max proceeded to explain his theory about Berrington and his bodyguard. When he was done, Mhi'ro called over one of his men and told him to bring a bottle of gaile and a glass. "Illuminating, to say the least."

Something in Mhi'ro's voice told Max that he was not at all surprised. The bottle came.

"Have a drink my boy," Mhi'ro said.

Max poured some liquor into the glass and took a drink. He smiled and waited.

"Your competitor Lazermore is playing out from the middle. He's working for the insurance people and for Berrington. The clever monster is pulling down more than twice what you earn in a year, plus a commission. It doesn't matter to him if the Turin Balls are sold or recovered. Now, I know the auction is happening tomorrow night in the underground near 42nd Street. Pir'na will get you the particulars. I want you to inform Lazermore, without informing Lazermore, about the meeting. I want you to be there too. Don't worry about Shera. He won't be a problem."

Max sat back. "I think Shera wants my skin."

Mhi'ro laughed. "That can be said of many who roam the streets of New Gate. I said don't worry, because he will be the one auctioning off the Turin Balls. He's no longer interested in killing you, because he got the cabinet from the boat and now wants to sell it for a mountain of roy bills. Berrington, along with some others, will be there to bid." Mhi'ro took a sip of his tree spice. "I know you have an honest streak in your core. Most disturbing, to be sure. You can tell your bronzie friend Detective Jonstone, but make sure he and his rabble arrive thirty minutes too late. You follow me? There is clan business I want addressed before they come crashing in."

Max nodded. "Ya, but I don't fully understand."

"You will," Mhi'ro said. "Now, beat it. Get a good night's sleep. Have dinner with that young female widow, Mrs. Tre'hu. Tomorrow all will become plain as the scales on your face."

Max downed his gaile. "I don't have scales."

"Nobody is perfect, Max," Mhi'ro replied.

Chapter 9

An Unexpected Mixer

MAX WANDERED OUT ONTO the street. His mind was whirling. Mhi'ro seemed reassuring, but something in his tone and posture caused Max to be concerned.

"Take it easy, he said," Max muttered to himself. "Have the bronze show thirty minutes late, he says." He found the first public vocalrelay box and dialed up the 20th Precinct. "Let me speak to Mrs. Tre'hu." A moment passed. "Limiric? You're in the clear. Return to your home. All the heat is turned way down for now. I'll be at your place in a few minutes. Okay. See you soon."

Max hailed a carriage, climbed in, and told the driver to take him to Limiric's. They cut through traffic and the park. On the other side, the carriage stopped. Max paid and got out.

He walked in a haze, muttering to himself all the way to Limiric's door. After pulling the long braided cord of the notice bell, he waited for a servant to open the front door. There was no answer.

Max stepped back and looked up at the windows of all four stories. One of the drapes fluttered and then became still. He pursed his lips, felt for his pistol, and started heading down to the walkway. He then made for the alley that led to the home's gardens.

He climbed the tall brick wall and landed in a winter-barren landscape with a hothouse and various deciduous trees bare of leaves. The snow was thin around the wall, but where the building's shadow lay, the snow was still thick and icy. There were footprints—the three-toed type.

Ahead, the kitchen door was ajar. Max opened it and slipped inside. A pair of grimalden boots sat by the portal leading into the main house. He went upstairs. The tread creaked as he went up. A slight hint of brimstone lingered in the air.

Max turned the corner at the top and found the door cracked open. He pushed, and the door slid over a thick red carpet. He pulled out his pistol, checked the rounds, and cocked the hammer. Max then moved slowly down the long hallway lined with columns.

He heard hushed voices coming from an open pocket door just ahead. Max moved into position and gripped the handle.

He jerked the door to the side, leapt in, and threw his back against the wall. The pistol was outstretched, ready for action.

Sitting on a couch were Limiric and Lazermore. Both cradled teacups and were startled by his entrance.

"Nice of you to join the party, Max," Lazermore said. "A bit late, and I see you forgot to bring anything other than your gun."

"Max, what are you doing?" Limiric called out. "Have you lost your mind?"

Max frowned, uncocked his weapon, and put it back in his pocket. "What are you two doing? What is he doing here?"

Limiric took a sip of her tea. "Mister Lazermore was just telling me about the recovery work he is doing, trying to find the cabinet my husband had."

"Oh, was he now?" Max narrowed his gaze at the daemon. "Sorry to tell you, my friend, the cabinet was broken and is now in the hands of Lightbox and his mob."

"You gave it to them?" Lazermore was annoyed.

"That's like asking a fish if he gave himself to the fisherman." Max stated. "It was a trade. One broken cabinet for mine and Limiric's lives. A valid trade, if you ask me."

"Those idiots will be auctioning it off as soon as they find a venue!" Lazermore stated.

"It's already set up, from what I hear. Somewhere in the underground off 42nd Street. I hear it's fetching quite a high bid already."

Lazermore stood. "My apologies." He bowed slightly. "I hope to take up your offer for lunch another time. I'm pressed to meet with my employer." He left quickly.

"Where's your servants?" Max asked gruffly.

"Today is Mar Tripping's Day. They have the day off." She stood up. "Now, will you kindly tell me what has happened?"

Max sat down. "It's all about Tararill's and your husband's murders. I'm not sure what Lazermore told you to gain entrance, but he is mixed up in it. How deep, I can't say yet. Tomorrow night is a secret auction where they plan to sell your husband's cabinet. I'm going to be there, and I know that

Lazermore and his patron will be too. The killer will also be there. I plan to have the murderer apprehended and maybe the lot of 'em thrown in the pen!" Max was showing his anger.

"Now what?" Limiric sat back down. "Come sit. Have some tea. We will figure this out together."

Max sat. "What did Lazermore tell you?"

"He told me that he works for the insurance company that my husband hired. He had a copy of a contract with Hemet's signature on it. He suggested that I stood to make a lot of money, but he needed to be sure the item was not in the house."

"Did he search the house?" Max was direct.

"A cursory search. Nothing was found." Limiric poured Max a cup of the tea, brought it over to him, and then sat back down.

"Something stinks in all of this. Let me think..." Max sipped his tea and sat back. "Do you have a ballroom dress?"

"Of course," Limiric replied.

"Let's take a little trip downtown for dinner." Max stood up.

MAX AND LIMIRIC ARRIVED at the Golden Polyglot just before the twenty-hundred-hours bell echoed from the temple chimes. The sound rained down over the tall surrounding buildings as he and Limiric reached the door.

"Hi, Max. What's the rumple? Do you have a reservation?" asked the gatekeeper.

"Something like that," Max said smoothly.

"Ah, yes. No worries, Max. Come this way." The gatekeeper handed them off to an elvish waiter, and they began to pass through the large ballroom, which was half dining room.

Once they were at their table, the waiter spread out a silk tablecloth and then placed the cutlery, glasses, and plates. In the middle was a three-tiered candleholder that bathed the table and its occupants in a soft yellow light.

Max tucked a twenty into the waiter's pocket and ordered drinks. By the time the drinks arrived, Max had found the first of his targets.

"There." Max pointed through the sea of heads at an elf standing tall. "Pip."

"Who's Pip?" Limiric asked.

"The one who I believe murdered Tararill and your husband." Max took a serious sip of his bright red Floundery Foundry, a drink that glowed like a burning ember. It was sweet and strong, and he nursed it as the night evolved.

"Why is he standing?" Limiric asked.

"He's a bodyguard for Mister Highloe Berrington, the city proctor for steam and electric contracts. He is sitting just to the right of Pip." Max took out his pipe and struck a match. He pointed to another part of the restaurant. "That's Pornet Lewis, the owner of the steam-rail business on the continent. That person over there." He pointed to a different area. "That's Silimet Noland. She controls the electric power industry in the Southern States." He looked about and then stopped. "Over there is Hubert Von Doceillonger, the gnome financier and banker from Iron Hills. I could throw a bread roll in any direction and hit someone bidding on the auction tomorrow," Max said.

"Powerful people," Limiric stated as she took a drink.

"More than that. In this room are most of the movers and shakers from the city and the continent. I can't believe I thought this was just about murder," Max mused.

Limiric took out a silver case and removed a smoke. A passing waiter quickly lit it for her and disappeared into the crowd. "So, what are you saying? Hemet was mixed up in some conspiracy?"

Max scanned the room. "These people are here for a single purpose, I'll bet. Look at them—prim and proper with armed guards and wads of money. They're the same sods that sent us off to war just a few years ago. The rich stink of the corpses they helped feed into those golden clouds of bullets and fire." He looked over at Limiric, who was staring at him with some concern. "Sorry. I still have a dagger in my heart about those muddy trenches." He took a sip from his glass.

"Why are we here really?" Limiric asked.

"To get an idea of what we're...I'm up against tomorrow night." Max lit his pipe. He looked back at Limiric. "And to have a nice meal."

They ate and talked into the night. As the band played, Max and Limiric danced on the ballroom floor. When they returned to their table, there was a visitor.

"You really belong on the walkway or gutter," said Pip.

Max sat down as if he had no cares. "Pip! What rotted log did you crawl out from under? I mean, where did Berrington dredge you up from?"

"He was my commander at the battle of Forgotten Ridge. Only eight of us lived that day. Now, only two." Pip stared with his one eye down at Max. "I can't decide if you're so brave that you're stupid, or you are so stupid you appear brave. Here is a little advice: stay away. Do the lady a favor and find another window to peep through. If you don't, the rats will be feeding on your bloated corpse, and your girl here will be slaving in a brothel somewhere in the Southern States." He turned and walked across the room back to Berrington.

"That guy just keeps getting more charming every time I meet him," Max quipped.

"He is terrifying," Limiric stated.

"Ya. I suspect he is terrifying in all aspects of his life. I'll not underestimate him." Max took another drink as he watched Pip. Pip looked over and stared for a moment. He then pointed at Max and then at himself, nodded, and smiled.

It was a threat, and Max knew Pip wanted nothing better than to kill him. The feeling was mutual.

Max checked his wrist-clock. "It's nearly zero two hundred. Let's call it a night."

They left through the front door, and Max caught a carriage. They traveled back into Goblin Town, and he escorted Limiric to her door.

"Will you stay?" she asked.

"Sorry, sugar, but I can't. There's somewhere I got to be before I can drop off, and you can't come with me. Don't worry. I'll come by in an hour or so. I can leave from here tomorrow night."

She sighed. "I'm scared, Max. All this has me frightened out of my wits."

"I get the feeling your part is done now. No reason for them to bother you. They got the cabinet, and neither of us are going to squawk to the authorities. Settle in, and I'll be back before you know it."

He flagged down a carriage. "Take me over to 42nd Street," Max said. The driver engaged the drive and blasted some steam around the front and sides. The machine drove out into the dark street.

Max walked into the Burning Soul Tavern. At the bar sat Pir'na. In front of him was a book of numbers, and he was thumbing through the pages as Max sat down.

"Hey, Pri'na. What's the flap?"

"Max, you're a busy chum-mucker. I take it you're here for a bit of info?"

Max frowned. "Ya. Mhi'ro sent me."

Pri'na tapped a finger on the bar. "Pony up first."

Max opened his wallet and put a twenty on the bar. Pri'na tapped three more times right on top of the bill.

"Really? You're going to make me pay eighty bills for info Mhi'ro sent me to get?"

"You ain't going to complain to Mhi'ro, are ya, Maxie?" Pri'na narrowed his eyes.

"Max frowned again and shelled out three more twenties. "There. I hope you at least offer me a comped glass of gaile."

"Comped?" Pri'na chuckled. "You just paid for it." He waved over the barkeep and had a bottle brought over. Without looking, he passed Max a paper and then stood up. "Listen, Max. Mhi'ro has his reasons for wanting you there. A little advice: keep the bronze a half hour late, and you can get out of all of this with more than your skin. You follow?" He looked Max directly in the eyes. Pri'na picked up the loose bills, turned, and walked into the back room.

Chapter 10

A Royal Screwing

MAX'S EYES SLOWLY CAME open. The light was bright. A bolt of terror ran up his spine, as he didn't recognize where he was. White drapes, tall bay windows, a white bed frame, and powder-blue sheets. His head was pounding, and he struggled to sit up.

Across from him, he saw a full-body mirror. His reflection was unflattering. He scooted back, leaned against the headboard, and took a deep breath. A strong smell of perfume floated in the air.

Limiric came into the room carrying a silver tray. She set it down, sat on the bed, poured out a cup of dark-black skull rush, and buttered two gnome breads studded with berries.

"You were a bit stewed when you came over. You're heavier than you look," she said.

"Sorry. I hope I didn't—"

"Not to worry. You were in no shape to embarrass yourself more than you did."

"What time?" Max asked.

"One thirty." She pointed at a clock sitting on the fireplace mantel. "I take it you're not going to let me come along tonight?"

"It would be an unnecessary risk," Max told her. "Too many things could go wrong. This is what you've paid me for—to take these risks."

She gave a weak smile and then nodded. "I understand. So, you don't think I can handle myself?"

"No. I know you can. I just couldn't live with myself if you were injured or killed. I prefer you alive." He smiled at her and then took a sip of the hythana. "Boy, that stuff sure clears the head!" He took a bite of the gnome bread. His stomach growled loudly.

"I had your clothes cleaned while you were asleep. They're hanging in the closet. Have a shower while you're at it." She stood up and headed for the door.

Max realized he did not smell good. "Ah, sorry for being like this." He stood and headed toward the washroom. She did not avert her eyes but took in the full visage of his filthy nude self.

"I'll be downstairs in the parlor," Limiric said and left the room.

MAX HIT THE STREET. It was already dark, and he had a good thirty minutes to get to 42nd Street. Goblin Town was buzzing with activity. He'd forgotten it was the Trevin Holiday, and most, if not all, of the food and festivities were paid for by Mhi'ro's mob.

He was nearly at the intersection when a steam carriage rolled up next to him.

"Hey, Maxie. We've been looking for you. Get in!" Lib'ro said out the window.

"You're hijacking me?" Max was surprised. His hand drifted toward his pocket.

"No. And the boss says you get to keep your popper on you tonight. We just needed to pick you up because there was a change in plans and location." The steam carriage stopped, and the door came open.

Max shrugged. He knew it could be that they were taking him to his death, but he climbed in anyway.

They drove around the south side of the park and then the driver took a righthand turn.

"We're going through the park?" Max asked. No one replied.

Somewhere among the glowing orbs of the lamps was an old steel door. Along the street were private carriages that had already been parked.

"It's underway?" Max asked.

Lib'ro only smiled.

Max was herded to a muscular human at the door. He nodded to Lib'ro, and they went in and down a winding metal stairwell.

Max heard the sound of an auctioneer. They came out into a large round space. In the middle were Shera, a few of his elves, an auctioneer, and the somewhat damaged cabinet from the boat.

Max was taken to Mhi'ro, and he stood quietly as the bidding continued. Across the way was Berrington and his protector, Pip. Every few moments, Pip would raise a red paddle and the auctioneer would call out a new price. Others were raising and lowering paddles as well.

"How much is it up to?" Max asked.

Mhi'ro's bodyguard leaned over. "Thirty-six million and a half Royal Bills."

"What's Mhi'ro's cut?" Max asked.

Pir'ro smiled but said nothing.

Max felt a sinking sensation in his stomach.

"Thirty-six five... Going once...twice!" the auctioneer shouted. "Thirty-seven... No, thirty-eight... Now thirty-nine..."

The tension was palpable. The competition was fierce. Max was feeling dizzy as the amount rose to fifty-three million. Then, it was over.

"Sold to Mister Berrington! Please bring up your payment now. Once paid, you can haul away your item," the auctioneer said.

Max peered through the crowd. He did not see William anywhere. Another sinking feeling came over him.

Berrington was beaming with satisfaction. Pip carried a brown leather satchel forward and set it on the auctioneer's podium. The man counted the bundles of money and then pronounced it legit.

Shera was nearly beside himself with joy. Max was sure the elf was planning all the ways he would spend the money.

The other guests, mostly grumbling, filed out. Max turned to leave, but Pir'ro grabbed his arm and shook his head. "We stay," he said.

Max knew that Jonstone was headed to the wrong location. If they were going to deal with him here, there would be no rescue by the bronze.

Berrington had two tough-looking fellows cart the cabinet out. As Pip was leaving, Berrington turned and spoke. "Sorry, old salt. Your services are no longer needed."

A host of powerful goblins parted, allowing Berrington to leave, but they closed up ranks, preventing Pip from leaving. The elf looked shocked and then backed into the middle of the room.

Shera looked surprised too. "What is this?"

The auctioneer took the sack of money and brought it over to Mhi'ro.

Guns were raised, and Shera, his henchmen, and Pip found themselves trapped. A hobgoblin ran over and disarmed the men then hastily got out of the line of fire.

"My elves will be down here in a minute if I'm not let out of here," Shera threatened.

Mhi'ro chuckled. "Shera, your crew are on a rail heading back down to the dock even as I speak. It's just you and me now."

Max could see the sudden serious concern in the elf's eyes.

"You disrespected me when you came into Goblin Town and worked over Max." Mhi'ro pointed at Max. "Poor fellow was under my protection, and you felt the need to piss all over my authority. Well, someone is going to have to pay for that."

A visible shiver ran up Shera's spine. "You can't touch me without the council's okay."

"True. So, I fine you your half of the transaction. The council has authorized that much. It's mine, you pointy-eared scab! Now take your men and get out of Goblin Town. From now on, you have to have my permission to come through, and if you don't, the council has given permission for me to deal with it the harder way."

Shera looked around. The goblin mobsters parted, and the elf and his cronies fled quickly. The mob closed up ranks again. Pip was alone.

"You!" Mhi'ro hissed. "You came into my town and murdered one of my employees. You're a nobody. There is no council that will save you. It is fitting that you will die down here. It is a pity that not all of your body parts are here to suffer."

A goblin came over with a truncheon and handed it to Max.

"Me?" Max asked, surprised.

"I think it fitting. You don't have to kill him, but I believe you have as much right to extract vengeance for Tararill as any of us. Do it for Tararill and Limiric. Do it for your self-respect," Mhi'ro told Max.

Max hefted the weapon and stepped into the circle. Pip smiled.

"Don't think that stick is going to help you," Pip said.

Max nodded. "Good point. You're a pretty good fighter." He pulled out his pistol and shot the elf in the leg. The pop was loud, echoing in the chamber.

Pip screamed, clutched the bloody wound, and fell to the ground. Mhi'ro laughed loud and long. Pip held his leg, groaning in agony.

"I should put a goldie in your damn head," Max growled.

There was a shout from somewhere down the tunnels.

"Looks like your friend Jonstone has arrived. I hope you don't regret not executing the fatherless scab," Mhi'ro said. "Don't worry about the bronze. I'll send someone to court who'll vouch you were somewhere else today."

Max looked around like a man fully confused. Mhi'ro put his hand on Max's shoulder.

"I can see in your face you don't get it. See, Maxie, you got to keep a few paces ahead of the competition. Shera has a rival, and this little dustup will make him appear weak in his family. His rival will keep him occupied and out of my business for a long while.

"Also, there is no Turin Balls magic machine." He chuckled. "Berrington got conned, I got his money, and he got a fancy case filled with a gas heater and lots of gears. When he realizes he has nothing to show for all the money he embezzled to buy it, he will belong to me. I own him now. Pip you can kill or let live if you want. Your friend the bronze will be here soon. I had one of my men call him with the location switch only after he got to 42nd Street. I needed to know for sure the bronze would be delayed the thirty minutes.

"I like you, Max. You're like the son I never had. You can choose to tell the bronze what we've done, and our friendship will vanish, or you can take this"—he held out a bundle of Royal Bills—"and take that lady friend of yours for a nice tropical vacation. Let the courts worry about what happens while you're gone. In the end, who knows who did what, where, and when? It's up to you."

Max looked at the money and then over at Pip. He took the bundle.

Mhi'ro laughed hard. "You're no fool, Max. I see a bright future for you." He left, followed by his son and bodyguard.

A moment later, Jonstone and the bronze came rushing in, their pistols drawn and truncheons held high. Pip was holding his leg, trying to keep it from bleeding out.

"Max!" Jonstone called. "How did you get here?"

"To be honest Nick, I am not sure. This elf is the one who killed Hemet Tre'hu and Tararill. You'll find the burns on his face consistent with the blowback from a peroxide misfire."

Jonstone pointed at Pip. "Arrest that elf!" A bronze rushed over and slapped cuffs on Pip. "Call a medic while you're at it."

"What happened down here?" Jonstone asked.

"I'm not really sure. All I can say is that no one was killed. You know, I really don't think I saw anything of note," Max said.

Jonstone called Sarack over. "Take his statement."

Max sat down and produced his pipe.

"What did you see, Max?" Sarack asked.

"Are you familiar with the Turin Balls?" Max questioned.

"I'm only concerned about these two low hangers," Constable Sarack said, grabbing his crotch.

Max made an expression of being caught off guard. "Really? Do they dangle around your feet when you're at the beach?"

Sarack chuckled. "They leave drag marks in the sand every time, Maxie old boy."

Max gave a small guffaw. "I'm not glad you shared that with me."

Sarack chuckled. "What are the Turin Balls?" Sarack asked.

"If you buy me a drink sometime—say, in a few months—I'll tell ya all about it."

Sarack smiled. "Sounds like a plan, Max. I hope they serve those double pints where we go. Now, what did you see down here? For the court...for the record."

WILLIAM MADE HIS WAY through the stacks of cargo, boxes, and sacks of grain. The warehouse was cold as the wind from the port blasted through the large open roller doors on either side. Just ahead, a man stood.

"Did you bring it?" asked the man.

"Of course. I provide the absolute best service when it comes to items of antiquity that serve powerful people," William said as he stopped and waited.

The man's stark white cape fluttered under his arm, and his white topper was tucked under the other. At his feet sat a simple cloth bag latched at the top with a brass clasp.

"Don't you want to know if I have all the money?" the man asked.

"Unthinkable!" William stated. "This business—my business—is predicated on trust. We both know what we are doing is illegal, but if you ever want to do business again within New Gate for magic relics, you know not to play nonsensical games, as do I."

The man laughed and then kicked the bag across the polished cement floor to William, who opened the sack and then closed it again.

From under his overcoat, William took a small box the length of his arm, set it on the ground, and slid it over to the man in white. A moment passed as the man examined the box.

"This is it?"

William remained calm. "It is. Open the top. You will see two nubs of differing metals on either side. Connect those to wires, as you would any powerful electrical device. You can test its output. I can tell you it is powerful."

The man in white opened the lid. He took a device out from his coat pocket and touched one lead to one peg and the other to the opposing metal stud. A broad smile grew across his face. "Almost impossible to believe," he said under his breath.

"If you don't mind me asking," William began, "what are your plans for the Turin Balls?"

"I intend to build a navy that will command the seas. I will bring shipping of supplies to its knees, and they will pay me a handsome commission to keep the ocean's goods flowing."

William chuckled. "Brilliant!"

"You are not concerned?" the man in white asked.

"Who am I to get between a fellow businessman and his endeavors? May the gods smile upon your enterprise." William picked up the sack of money.

The man in white laughed again. "You are a remarkable fellow. Let me know if you come across anything else that might stimulate my interest. Contact me the same way as before." He turned and walked out of the warehouse to a waiting motor launch. He climbed aboard, and the craft headed out into the harbor toward a yacht that was weighing its anchor.

"A pleasure doing business," William said quietly as he made for the nearest steam carriage.

MAX AND LIMIRIC SAT in folding chairs under a colorful umbrella on the white-sand beach. The heat of the sun was becoming a bit too intense for him to sit still, so he stood and headed for the water.

"So, it was all just a con job?" Limiric asked.

"Yup! Concocted by the mob to bilk the city out of a few million bills."

"Does it bother you at all?"

Max chuckled. "A little. But the killer of your niece and husband is in the stripy box, and he rolled over on his boss, who is in there now too. All punished, and we got a nice vacation out of it. I count it as a win–win all the way around."

Limiric sipped her cold drink, stood up, and took Max by the hand. She pulled him along until they were waist-deep in the shallow surf as the emerald-green waves crashed lazily along the shore of the lagoon. Both plodded about the seashore for a while. As night came, they drank and danced, which continued until dawn.

After they returned to their room at the inn, Max peeled off his clothes and fell into bed. As he waited for Limiric to come back from the washroom, Max stretched his arms toward the ceiling, put his hands behind his head, and declared, "This sure is living."

Don't miss out!

Visit the website below and you can sign up to receive emails whenever Lawrence BoarerPitchford publishes a new book. There's no charge and no obligation.

https://books2read.com/r/B-A-MRTR-VFOYC

BOOKS 2 READ

Connecting independent readers to independent writers.

Did you love *Goblins, Dames, Booze & Bullets*? Then you should read *Memoirs from a Parallel Universe; Jake and the Treasure of Solomon Lake*[1] by Lawrence BoarerPitchford!

Jake "Facebreaker" Sharkar lives his life between the lines of law-and-order and outright villainy. Fresh from committing murder, he finds that his employer has a proposition for him.

Instead of paying him for his work, Jake has the opportunity to help find and share in the profits if he helps recover the lost treasure of Solomon Lake.

Not even wandering aliens will keep Jake from garnering glory and promised wealth. Make no mistake, it is unwise to double-cross a man like Jake. And, for those who thought they could, they have another thing coming.

Ride through the Host Systems and beyond, as Jake searchesthe galaxy for a fabled cache of alien artifacts looted and lost hundreds of years earlier by the maverick explorer Solomon Lake - that mythological pioneer, miner, and wild-man, who flew by the seat of his pants and lived a life of a libertine - After all, who doesn't want to be a libertine?. Buckle up - it's blastoff time.

Read more at https://www.boarerpitchford.com.

Also by Lawrence BoarerPitchford

Augerland Series
Harrow's Gate

In The World Of Hyboria
The Last Atlantean Prince

Memoirs from a Parallel Universe
Memoirs from a Parallel Universe; Jake and the Treasure of
Solomon Lake
Memoirs from a Parallel Universe; The Cox Head Horror
Goblins, Dames, Booze & Bullets
The Leftover World
Sala The Acolyte

Standalone
Thadius

Watch for more at https://www.boarerpitchford.com.

About the Author

Author Lawrence BoarerPitchford creates and publishes fiction in many genres. From humble beginnings to worldwide author, Lawrence has carved out a niche in the area of fictional works. Barbarian fantasy, classic fantasy, science fiction, historical fiction, and horror/thriller, he has created many memorable worlds, characters, and stories.

Read more at https://www.boarerpitchford.com.